Ten Tall Tales
And Twisted Limericks

Ten Tall Tales

And Twisted Limericks

Edited by Ian Whates

NewCon Press
England

First edition, published in the UK September 2016
by NewCon Press

NCP 105 (hardback)
NCP 106 (softback)

10 9 8 7 6 5 4 3 2 1

ISBN: 978-1-910935-25-5 (hardback)
978-1-910935-26-2 (softback)

Cover art copyright and front cover design © 2016 by Sarah Anne Langton
Back Cover Design by Ian Whates
Text layout by Storm Constantine

Contents

Ten Tall Tales

An Introduction

Ian Whates

At some point in 2015 I sat down and started to consider how best to mark NewCon Press' tenth anniversary in 2016 (ten years, *really*? How the heck did that happen?). In the early days, NewCon's output consisted exclusively of anthologies – I love a good short story, me – so of course there would have to be an anthology... or two... or three...

Presumably it must have seemed a good idea to my 2015 self to schedule twice as many titles for 2016 as in any previous year. With the benefit of hindsight, I'd like to travel back in time twelve months and give my past self a slapping.

Not that I haven't loved working on the three (and a half) anthologies, you understand. The first two (and a half) enabled me to feature many of the authors who have supported NewCon throughout the past decade – Adam Roberts, E.J. Swift, Adrian Tchaikovsky, Jaine Fenn, Eric Brown, Nina Allan, Gavin Smith, Una McCormack, Neil Williamson, Mercurio D. Rivera, Donna Scott, and Tim C. Taylor among them, while also working with several authors, who are new to NewCon, both established and less familiar: Peter F. Hamilton, Nancy Kress, Ian McDonald, Genevieve Cogman, Tade Thompson, Janet Edwards, Nik Abnett, Christopher Nuttall, Jack Skillingstead, J.A. Christy, Allen Stroud, and Bryony Pearce included...

So why the need for a further anthology?

Because, great though these first two (and a half) volumes are, they haven't told the full story. *Crises and Conflicts* is all about military SF and space opera, *Now We Are Ten* takes a broader approach to science fiction and genre, and *X Marks the Spot* is as much non-fiction and stats as it is about fiction; so what about the darker side? What about stories that unsettle and cause the reader to glance warily into dark corners or imagine a gentle breath on the back of their neck when there's no one else around? What about the horror, the dark fantasy and science fiction? Well, for all of that, we have *Ten Tall Tales and Twisted Limericks*.

As with the earlier volumes, it's a pleasure to work once again with such astute observers of the darker aspects of humanity as Sarah Pinborough, James Barclay, Maura McHugh, Edward Cox, Simon Clark, Paul Kane, Andrew Hook, and Mark West, and to welcome others to NewCon's pages for the first time: Ramsey Campbell, Michael Marshall Smith, and Lynda E. Rucker.

So here it is, the third and final full volume of fiction celebrating NewCon's tenth birthday: ten stories that veer from dark crime to shocking horror, from mystical portent to breathless combat in alien realms, from a man struggling to come to terms with the sins of his past to woman striving to accept the implications for her present... All punctuated by limerickal interludes courtesy of Ramsey Campbell.

This is a book I'm proud of. A book I hope you enjoy.

Here's to the next ten years.

Ian Whates
Cambridgeshire
August 2016

To The Power Of...

Paul Kane

The ferry rocked again as the waves rose and fell.

It matched the movement of his stomach, the feeling in his guts that had forced him on deck in case he needed to throw up. Charles Mansfield clutched the railing again as another huge wave battered the vessel.

"Are... are you okay, Inspector?"

It was a stupid question – quite clearly he was not – but Mansfield appreciated the thought. He looked to his right, where a fresh-faced young officer called... Stewart, if he remembered correctly, was watching him with concern. Christ, he couldn't even remember what it was like to be that young – that innocent. Certainly not since he joined – was headhunted by – the SCI. He'd seen things in that time which would turn most men's hair white in seconds, then cause it to fall out; a different kind of headhunting altogether (literally in one particular investigation). And though he had only just turned 40, he felt about 100; those years gone now, forever.

Mansfield held up a hand and nodded a couple of times – although that didn't do much for the way he felt. When the uniformed man just stood there, gaping, he clarified this with: "I'm fine." He managed to wait until the man had turned away before putting a hand to his mouth, stemming the rising bile – which coincided with yet another upswing of the ferry.

Wasn't just the seasickness that was causing his stomach to lurch, however, it was the thought of this mercy dash they were on, a life or death race across this stretch of sea. The thought of what might be waiting at the other end for him and the handful of men he'd managed to round up on such short notice during the holiday period.

And those thoughts brought back others – about the case, about how all this had started. About how he'd got too close to things at one point, and about how he'd failed all those people. Failed *her*. How he was determined not to fail again; that would at least go some way to making things right… though not much.

Mansfield fought down the queasiness, but wasn't able to do the same with the memories. They came crashing back as hard as the sea was pummelling their craft.

The first one, he hadn't been around for, of course. In fact it had pretty much gone under the radar, had almost been missed. Mainly because it had been a John Doe, a homeless person living rough on the streets of New York. Police there had looked into the matter but hadn't really given it top priority – and you couldn't actually blame them. Didn't flag as suspicious at first; it just looked as if he'd died of a combination of exposure under that bridge in a freezing cold winter and alcohol poisoning, the empty bottle of meths lying not too far away from the body. Open and shut case…

Only it wasn't – far from it. The authorities there wouldn't have even made the connection if there hadn't been a second one, this time a lawyer called Melanie Frakes who was just starting to make a name for herself in the windy city of Chicago. Sadly, the way she was making that name had caused more waves than Mansfield was currently enduring. Going after people who were known to have links to organised crime, hitching her wagon to a hotshot DA's star for a fast-track to the big time.

Instead, all it had got her was a fast-track to the morgue.

A single bullet to the back of the head at close range, as she was entering her apartment. Textbook execution-style killing, the detectives had said at the time. Only there were certain… curiosities. The missing finger, for instance, and the mark. A mark that Mansfield would become intimately acquainted with.

Hallmarks, it was thought, of a new assassin on the block; someone who could get the job done quickly and efficiently but left a calling card of sorts. The middle finger on the left hand he'd taken, was that some kind of message to the police, perhaps – flipping them the bird? Though wouldn't the killer have actually *given* it to them rather than making off with it? But the mark – the *brand* that identified Melanie as a target, that was something else.

The ME had discovered the mark when doing his autopsy; it was only small but it was there. Burned onto the flesh after the murder, a single letter 'X' on her shoulder. They'd speculated that he'd done this to show that the woman was now an *ex*-lawyer; a warning to halt the investigation into such dangerous people. It had scared the DA enough for him to go into hiding under an assumed name, never to be seen or heard from again. Mission accomplished, then.

Only somebody somewhere made the connection; a morgue attendant from New York who was an old school buddy of one of the cops working Melanie's case. The homeless man, the John Doe, well, he'd been missing a finger and he had the mark. They'd assumed back then that his digit (the first finger on the right hand) had been missing a while, something that had happened on the streets. And they'd thought the 'X', which on that occasion was located on his calf, was a birthmark. They hadn't really been looking for anything else. So no photos had been taken, nothing really recorded about that – and the body had already been incinerated; there was only so much room in the morgue and the Grim Reaper had been particularly busy that winter.

But the attendant remembered and he told his friend.

There had been some rumblings about looking into a possible connection but it never really went any further. As far as the Chicago PD were concerned they had their motive, they had people they were looking at for this – pin something on the family who were responsible for hiring the hitman, you might *find* the hitman – and that was that. Besides, there was a power struggle going on between rival factions in the city, whipped up by all this attention, which was pretty much occupying most of their time.

So the whole thing was swept under the carpet – not intentionally, it had to be said, just forgotten about.

Until LA. Until a nightclub owner called Brandon Palmer was killed as well. Alone and up in his office above his club, *Hotwings*, it happened in the early hours of a Saturday morning while the place was chock full to capacity, according to witnesses. Palmer had retired to take care of some business, he'd told his manager, but would be down later on to take care of a different sort – which usually involved him ushering two or three choice ladies upstairs. When the evening finally drew to a close and he hadn't ventured down again, his manager had gone to see if everything was okay.

It wasn't. Brandon Palmer had been garrotted, left sprawled over his desk on his back, head lolling over the edge with an expression of surprise still plastered across his features. The little finger of his left hand was gone, a fresh cut that had left blood splattered all over the papers he'd been perusing, creating miniature Rorschach tests for his discoverer to find. When the ME examined the body he found a small 'X' burned onto the skin on Palmer's side.

Officers trawled through CCTV footage but saw nobody entering the private chambers apart from the owner himself. Whoever had gained entrance and done this must have come in through the skylight on the roof, they reasoned, exiting the same way. But they could find no trace of any interloper, no forensic evidence of any kind, in fact.

There was no denying the link this time – it was too blatant. But because of the club's connection with drugs, the authorities returned to the theory that this was a hired assassin and he'd left his calling card again. Someone had wanted Palmer out of the picture for whatever reason, and somebody else had obliged. Whoever you wanted bumped off, they could make them an ex-person.

But why kill a tramp with no ties to anyone? And why take

those fingers…? It made no sense. Unless, as one Federal Agent called Edmonds – who was looking into the affair – posited, they were dealing with a serial murderer. Same MO each time, same markings: an X, as in crossing victims off? A trophy taken from each crime scene…

Mansfield recalled talking to Edmonds, asking him why he'd made that particular leap; the only person to have done so in those first few months.

The man had oddly hawk-like features – crooked nose and beady eyes. He'd frowned, as if to say it had been obvious. "It just seemed… I don't know, I just got a sense about it. Different methods of killing, yes – and we still have no way of knowing how the original vic was murdered now, or if indeed he even *was* – but the 'X', the missing fingers. A hitman wouldn't bother with all that, they'd be long gone. This was somebody who wanted something from his kills, and wanted people to *know*."

Sitting opposite him in that office in Washington, Mansfield had nodded and made a mental note to put this man's name forward to the powers that be; skills like that were treasured at the SCI, not ignored. Skills like his own.

Once the idea had been floated, it had been a case of everyone claiming to have thought it was a serial crime all along – and Edmonds had gradually been squeezed out of the frame. He didn't appear bitter about that, though, probably because the investigation had got nowhere anyway. "They did what they did," he'd told Mansfield. "I moved on."

Definitely SCI material.

Of course, Mansfield was coming to all this after the fact. He'd been given access to the files, to all the relevant material – one of the benefits of working for the group he was a part of – but that wasn't the same as being at the crime scenes himself. Not the same at all.

For one thing, all three of these killings had taken place a good nine years ago. He'd still been a DS then in Her Majesty's police force, hadn't even heard of the Serial Crime Initiative (most people *still* hadn't). There were times, dark times when he'd wake at 3 a.m., pillows and sheets drenched in sweat from a nightmare, that he wished *he'd* never heard of them. Yet there he was, thinking of putting someone like Edmonds forward.

Mansfield shook his head, swayed with the motion of the ferry. Dragged his mind back on track. If he was going to replay events from the start, then he needed to stick with it, go through it bit by bit. Even –

No. Not yet. Nine years ago…

The people looking into these cases had only joined the dots in retrospect, thanks to Edmonds' help, but it hadn't done them much good. They'd managed to come up with silly names, naturally; that was the one thing they'd excelled at. The cases were labelled 'X-Files', the victims 'X-Men' (and one 'X-Woman'). The killer: Ray.

"You know," one obnoxious police captain had explained to him, "like an 'X-Ray', Chuck."

"I get it," Mansfield had informed him, then said: "Please don't ever call me that again."

"'Course, when he reached three, we also called him Triple X – after that film with that fella. Oh, what's his name now…?"

"It's not really relevant," Mansfield had said with a world-weary sigh, though he knew the captain was trying to think of Vin Diesel, knowledge that would certainly not help them to catch the individual who'd been doing this – for it was starting to look like the same person, in spite of the spread of attacks.

Triple X. That was as far as they'd got back then; probably because it had been the last case that they knew of. Turned out they were wrong. Turned out there had been at least two more, this time in two other countries – although Mansfield wouldn't come across those until he started investigating it all himself.

Wind back a few months, to when he'd been tasked with looking into the slaughter of a gallery worker called Phillipa Attaway in Dublin. She'd been killed and arranged very much in the style of a painting called *Temptation* by a rising star in the art

world called Andrew Croft. In the painting, a semi-naked woman
has her left hand outstretched as if luring in a would-be suitor,
her right curled into a fist – the backdrop one that would rapidly
become synonymous with Croft, that of colourful shapes like
squares and circles, the inspiration from the surrealist movement
very much apparent.

Phillipa had been staged in the same manner as the woman in
Croft's piece, down to the clothing and the way her hair was
pinned back. Her neck had also been twisted, mirroring how the
woman's head was turned away; on backwards almost. Attaway's
co-workers had found her when they came to open up on the
Saturday – one of their busiest days at the gallery – and raised the
alarm. It wasn't long before it came to the attention of the SCI,
who had been investigating a series of killings where the
murderer seemed to be using this kind of thing as a jumping-off
point – creating their own 'works of art' with human bodies –
though the trail had recently gone cold.

Mansfield had been dispatched to look into the Attaway case,
and was given all the co-operation by the Gardaí he could have
wanted – in spite of the fact the Chief he liaised with there,
Byrne, had never come across the Initiative. He was more than a
little intrigued by it, though.

"A cross-border, international division, you say?" He rubbed
his bearded chin. "Interesting."

"And we'd appreciate any help you can give us with this one,"
Mansfield had said, genuinely meaning it.

"Of course, of course."

He was glad the man had said that, because he was sick of
pissing contests, to be honest – Supers throwing their weight
around, marking their territory, when they were all in this fight
together... and besides, it only ever took a few phone calls to
force people to play nicely. Never led to a comfortable working
environment, but then Mansfield wasn't in this to feel
comfortable, was he?

Thankfully, Byrne had seen the benefits of working with the

SCI from the get-go without any of the need for that nonsense – and within an hour of flying in, Mansfield was taken to see the body now that forensics had finished at the scene; and the inspector was given the file, including pictures, to peruse on his way to the morgue.

They were the kind of pictures he was used to after six years in this job, and several years before it in the ordinary police – the kind of images he'd seen time and again, both frozen in time like this or live at the scene. But his lip still curled at the sight, at the loss of human life; gone forever. That this poor woman had been the plaything of some psycho, trying to say something, to do something that was apparent just to them... These were the only images there were, because the person who had done this had somehow interfered with the CCTV footage both outside and inside the gallery – scrambled the pictures so you could barely see what was there; Mansfield knew of several ways of doing this, he'd encountered them before. Ways to screw with the tech that made everyone feel so safe these days. "We're here," the driver told him, snapping him out of his reverie.

By the time Mansfield was in that stark, sterile room, they'd made the discovery. An 'X' burned into Mrs Attaway's skin (and yes, she was married, with children he'd been told, so there was the knock on effect there to the family). "See, here," said the female pathologist who was masked so effectively only her eyes could be seen. She was pointing to Phillipa's left thigh, one of the areas that had been covered up at the crime scene to match Croft's painting. Mansfield, his own mouth covered over with a mask, bent and peered at the mark – which was a couple of inches or so in size. "Quite a bit of heat needed to generate a brand of that kind," offered the woman, "and definitely done post-mortis. As was this…"

Now she picked up Mrs Attaway's arm with latex-encased hands, lifting it and showing Mansfield her hand. The missing little finger on her right hand, to be precise; that too had been missed initially, because the hand had been bent into a ball.

"Severed expertly, probably snipped off with some form of shears." The woman who looked a bit like a spaceman brought two of her own fingers together in a cutting motion.

Mansfield frowned. Something about all this rang a bell, and it had absolutely nothing to do with the art serial killings he'd been sent there originally to explore. No, Mansfield soon began to realise that was just a smokescreen; to throw them off track and cover up something else even more effectively than the pathologist's flesh.

When he returned to his temporary HQ at the Dublin Met, where they'd put him up in an office of his own, complete with computer and access to the net, the first thing he'd done was log into the SCI database remotely. They'd been compiling this since before he joined them, from day one as far as he knew, connected to the main police databases around the world – just part of the interlinked way in which they worked – and certain key words like 'X' and 'finger' yielded quick results.

Within seconds, Mansfield was looking at details about the New York Homeless vic, about the lawyer Melanie Frakes, and about nightclub owner Brandon Palmer. Case notes from the past that might help him make sense of the present – and the future.

But there were two more examples that had been overlooked from that time. The first was a florist called Linda Nilsson from Stockholm, who had the back of her head caved in on the way to her car after shutting up shop. Her boyfriend, one Leppe Berg, apparently jealous because she'd started seeing another man, was thought to be responsible for the murder – indeed, they'd even found traces of her blood on his clothes when they'd discovered his own body at the home they shared: veins slit with a razor blade. The odd thing about it was that Linda was also missing a finger, the ring finger on her right hand – which was never found – and what looked like a small 'X' was discovered on the sole of her foot, though they hadn't really been sure it was burned in. Like the homeless man, they'd assumed it was a weird birthmark or something. Even if they had connected the death to those others, and thought that this was the same man – Triple... now Quadruple X – then at least he was dead and they could close the cases for good.

If only they'd also known about the other one in Australia, a man called Tom Spicer who went missing on a drive through the country's Red Centre of desert roads. His car was found abandoned on the Explorer's Highway – his engine had simply packed up – and by the time they found his body, after he'd got lost in the desert, it was in a terrible mess; pecked at by carrion, chewed by wild animals. The autopsy did, however, mention a missing first finger on his left hand and a mark that looked a little like an 'X' – though it was hard to tell for sure. In any event, these matters were not linked to any of the others and it was written off as an accidental death. Mansfield wasn't so sure, especially now that they had Mrs Attaway's body on their hands as well.

You could also rule out some kind of copycat, because it had been hard enough linking all these cases together when you were police, let alone digging around on your own. Nothing of any great significance had been released to the press, either (certainly not the finger business) and by the time anyone was starting to think about 'Triple' as a serial killer, the whole thing suddenly died down – and media attention had moved on to the next piece of news. A flash in the pan... Unless you were Linda Nilsson or Tom Spicer, of course.

Mansfield was beginning to have a very bad feeling about all this, and whenever that happened it usually meant the murders were linked. So what were they dealing with: a serial killer taking trophies – as Edmonds would eventually confirm when Mansfield took the trip over to the states, reviewing *all three* of the original cases – but what was the significance of the fingers?

All were spaced far enough apart in terms of location so as not to alert the respective authorities – after the original trio, anyway, which were at least in the same country – and now spaced far enough apart timewise, because they'd only just started up again.

Five killings back then, and one now? A gap of so many years… Maybe the culprit, who he had a hard time believing was Leppe Berg (more likely that he was just another way to throw them off the scent), had been placed in jail for a different offence? It would certainly explain why this little project had ground to a halt back then.

But what was going on with the Xs? Branding them, marking the spot of the victories, the treasures? If it was the latter, had the killer left something behind for later? Or *were* they simply crossing off these random victims – and these were completely random, as far as Mansfield could make out; nothing tying them together at all – in the same way you'd cross off items from a shopping list? A kill list? It was a terrifying thought – and with no way to predict the next one, nor any uniform or unifying method of dispatching the poor unfortunates, that made his job all the harder.

Near enough impossible, actually.

But he'd ordered the body of Mrs Attaway to be sent to London anyway, with a promise that she'd be delivered back to her family as soon as possible – and that he'd keep Byrne in the loop (as much because he'd been so helpful as it was a professional courtesy; it never hurt to foster good relations with the people you might end up working with down the line). Then, while his men did their thing, he jetted off to talk to police in Sweden, the USA and Australia… It had been a long few months, especially arranging for any of the bodies that remained – three had been cremated – to be exhumed, and by the time he was getting ready to return there was yet more news about the resurfaced X killer.

Not to mention another dead body.

No sooner had Mansfield's feet touched the ground at Heathrow than he was being whisked off to Cardiff, where a fresh crime scene was waiting for him.

"Only just happened, sir," this driver told him – one he was more familiar with, a young DC called Troughton, with a skin complaint and a smart mouth. "Quite a juicy one. It was flagged pretty much right away. Orders were given not to touch a thing until you arrived, but, well, I think there was some confusion so…"

Mansfield, jetlagged and irritable, had mumbled something – then snapped when the DC asked the inspector to repeat himself: "I said you'd better step on it, then!"

The driver had shut up, nodded and stamped on the accelerator as ordered. But the traffic had other ideas and seemed to hamper them every step of the way as they headed south west to Wales' capital.

Finally, they made it to the house in question – located on a small estate just outside Cardiff, where it was pelting down with rain. "Bit of a mess in there, I heard," said the DC, having assumed enough time had passed that he could engage Mansfield once more. "Really went to town."

He ignored the DC and climbed out of the car as soon as it had stopped, in spite of the terrible weather. Approaching the tape cordoning off the scene, he flashed his warrant card and asked to see the person in charge.

Mansfield was made to wait while a PC trotted off to fetch the Senior Investigating Officer. He grumbled as the rain drenched him, not really helping his mood. When the well-built detective deigned to put in an appearance, Mansfield could tell he was going to be trouble. The man was practically sneering at him as he said: "DCI Kendrick – and you are?"

"Mansfield, Serial Crime Initiative. I understand my people have been in touch."

"Never heard of them."

Mansfield sighed. *I'm going to have to make those calls, aren't I?* he thought to himself. *Meanwhile, Christ knows what's going on inside that house, the evidence that might be…*

"Look, we'd appreciate any assistance with –"

"And I'd appreciate it if you'd go off and mind your own bloody business. This is an active crime scene. *My* crime scene."

He was probably thinking this would be a career-defining case; people like him often did.

Mansfield gritted his teeth, breathed in and out a few more times. "I'm aware that it's a crime scene and of its nature. That's *why* I'm here, Chief Inspector – and this *is* my business, trust me."

The sneering man stared at him, then looked him up and down. "Show me something in writing and you can come inside."

"Oh for God's sake, man! I've just got off a plane, having spent a good deal of time looking into cases that could very well relate to the one inside and…"

The DCI walked off, actually walked away and left him. Mansfield's phone was out even before the man reached the door. Within the space of a few minutes, and much to the chagrin of that SIO – whose glare had trailed him even as he put on protective booties and gloves – Mansfield was inside and scrutinising the scene.

'Mess' and 'went to town' barely even covered it. The living room of the house was a bloodbath, red everywhere. And in the centre of the room, stripped down to his underpants and also covered in crimson, was the latest victim. Even if there wasn't the mark, which was larger and on his forehead – seemingly the only part of him that hadn't been stabbed or sliced – and the ring finger of the left hand hadn't been missing, there would have been no denying the connection to that recent murder in Ireland. For one thing the killer had painted crosses all over the walls in there with the victim's own blood.

If it wasn't their perp, Mansfield would be amazed.

"Name?" he had asked bluntly.

Kendrick said nothing in reply, was still sulking, so it was left to one of his junior officers to answer in his stead: "Alwyn Yates, graphic designer… Works from home, apparently."

"Who found him?"

"The girlfriend, one Briallen Arthur. They don't live together, so she was calling to cook him some dinner. Hell of a shock… Paramedics had to take her in because she was having some sort of panic attack by the time we got here."

Mansfield gave a nod. They'd do what they could for her, which was more than they'd be able to do for this poor bastard.

"So all this relates not only to the murder over in Ireland of that woman in the gallery, but others?" Kendrick suddenly piped up. Of course, why wouldn't he know about the previous one, if they'd been alerted at the SCI – but the others… Mansfield was beginning to wish he'd kept his mouth shut. It was the kind of rookie mistake he would have bollocked someone else for, the kind he might have expected from someone like Troughton. But he was tired – not just physically, but of the hunt. There was just so much he didn't understand and that made his head hurt. "Very interesting," Kendrick said with a grin.

He was the kind of person who'd start digging into it, the kind who – when Mansfield snatched all this away from him, which he had every intention of doing – would be looking to cause trouble. Would be looking for some kind of retaliation.

Mansfield had no way of knowing for certain, of course, whether it was Kendrick who'd fed it to the media, had given them a couple of crumbs which some investigative reporter then made a meal of, but either way he'd only just returned to London – having made arrangements for Yates' remains to follow him – when news broke that the X Killer was back.

Mansfield had been in the incident room at SCI home base, 'The Factory' in London, when he received the news. He'd been staring at boards with photos on them, the victims connected with red lines, but very little else to link them together. Not even their ages, the last two being significantly older than the first handful. The only patterns seemed to be the branding, the missing fingers and the fact that the murders had occurred "boy, girl, boy, girl…" Which mean that they could probably expect the next one to be a woman.

When he got the phone call to tell him what was happening, Mansfield immediately switched on the TV and went to a random news channel. Sure enough, he caught the end of one report:

"…apparently linked to crimes that took place several years ago. But now the murderer has struck again in Ireland and Wales, leaving behind a symbol in the shape of a letter 'X'."

"Shit!" was all Mansfield could muster. This would set the investigation back no end.

Over the coming weeks, with enquiries being funnelled through to them from all over the country and beyond, they had to sift through so many timewasters. Whether it was by luck or design, the nature of how the X was left behind by the killer hadn't been uncovered – nor had the information about the missing digits, so they were still able to rule out a lot of the crackpots claiming to either be 'Mr X' – which was the media's new stupid name for their killer – or know about them.

There were the usual copycats as well, sad to say. A handful of victims they'd thought might be down to their perp, but were instead murdered by nutjobs who were easily traced and picked up by local police. Not much comfort for the victims or the relatives, it had to be said. Loved ones: gone forever.

Mansfield ground his teeth together again as he recalled attending one such crime scene just outside Norwich – where the victim, a man called Larry Groves, had been killed with an axe and had an X drawn on him in marker pen; all his fingers intact. Neighbours had heard the noise and called the police, who'd picked up a guy dressed in black trackies and a hoodie running away from the scene. On that occasion it had been a patient from the local psychiatric facility who'd been released a little too early due to governmental budget cuts, and had become fascinated by the idea of Mr X… To such an extent he'd wanted to *become* that man; to give his own life some sort of purpose.

Kendrick certainly had a lot to answer for, if it was him – and Mansfield vowed that he'd definitely be looking into the situation more closely once he was finished with all of this shitstorm. Then whoever had leaked to the press would wish they'd never been born.

So it was with a certain weariness Mansfield welcomed the

news that someone had come forward with more information – not least because he hadn't had much sleep since returning from his trip: a combination of his body clock still not having adjusted and nightmares about that blood-soaked room in Wales.

"Can this wait until tomorrow?" he'd asked, catching his exhausted reflection in the glass of his office, his curly, dark brown hair generously flecked with grey; rubbing his forehead and transferring his mobile to his other ear.

"I think you're going to want to meet with this person as soon as possible, sir," said the sergeant at a station in the Midlands where the woman had handed herself in; patched through to him because of the nature of the call. "Reckons she's next on the victim list and can prove it."

Mansfield's ears had pricked up at that one, and he'd sent for Troughton to take him up north as quickly as possible.

When they arrived, the inspector had been buzzed in and taken through the corridors in that station, escorted by the man he'd spoken to on the phone. "She was in a hell of a state, I can tell you," he assured Mansfield. "Agitated, shaking. One of our lads made her a nice cup of sweet tea to calm her down."

"Thank you, Sergeant," said Mansfield, as he was led to the door of the interview room where the woman in question was being held. He stood on his toes and peered inside, through the glass in the door.

She had long, dark hair – pretty, but not in an obvious way. When she sipped at the tea, Mansfield saw that her eyes were red raw as if she'd been crying. The woman was wearing a jumper, with jeans – her coat and scarf slung over the back of the chair she was sitting on. There was a uniformed officer inside the room with her, not because they thought she might be a threat at all, but probably because they were worried about her state of mind. Mansfield himself was still wondering whether she was one of the crazy brigade, the latest in a long line of people who were muddying the waters – but not a killer, this one. Somehow he knew that; *felt* it.

Fingers outstretched, he hesitated before opening the door – but then sheer habit took over and suddenly he was inside with her. The woman flinched when she heard the handle turn, and for that he somehow felt guilty. He hadn't meant to startle her.

He was about to apologise when he realised how ridiculous that would sound, so introduced himself instead, holding out a hand as she rose. "Inspector Mansfield, Serial Crime Initiative."

"Joanna," she answered, taking his hand and shaking it; the skin there was cold, almost freezing. "Joanna Hutchings...or at least..." She shook her head, but refused to explain when he looked confused, so Mansfield simply carried on regardless.

"I'm told you might have some information that will help with our enquiries?" The standard patter; and this wasn't an interrogation.

"I..." She shook her head again and Mansfield stretched out his hand, motioned for Joanna to take her seat again. He dismissed the uniformed officer – wouldn't be needed now, plus the less people who were privy to this the better – and then took his own seat opposite her, across the table provided. Mansfield took out his phone, asked if it was all right for him to record their conversation – to which she nodded.

"So...?" Mansfield prompted.

"You're going to think I'm being... It's just that, I think I know who's been committing those murders." *Here we go,* thought the inspector. "You see, I used to know him." *Right, you and dozens of other people; and we've had to listen to the lot of them.* "We all did."

Mansfield snapped to. "All... as in...?"

"The... Well, the other people he killed."

"You knew Phillipa Attaway, Alwyn Yates?"

She shook her head this time, then clarified. "I... yes, but they weren't called that then."

"Weren't called...?"

"They had different names. So did the others."

"The others..."

"From before." She sighed, took another sip of tea. "Look,

it's hard to explain, but we were chosen."

"They were, yes. By the killer." *Victims usually are*, Mansfield thought to himself; then: *easy... go easy.*

She shook her head, then nodded again – adding to the confusion. "He's not a killer... at least not in the way you think he is."

It was Mansfield's turn to sigh. "I'm sorry, you've lost me."

"We were selected, yes. Back when we were very young... didn't know any better."

Chosen, selected... headhunted. It was all the same thing.

"I... I suppose we were all looking for something, as you are back then. Some kind of purpose? Guidance." Joanna looked him directly in the eye, as if realising she'd missed out some vital bit of this. "We were all at university, Inspector. Studying different things, but he drew us together. Became our mentor. Our... master. Taught us about... about the power."

"Who did?" he asked, leaning forward, suddenly very interested. This was ringing more than a few warning bells; in fact this was starting to sound like a cult to him.

"It's hard. I'm struggling to... This stuff has only recently started coming back to me," she explained, with a half smile. For some reason he felt like offering her one back. "He... he called himself Carlo, I think. No, *De* Carlo. He was older than us, in his thirties, maybe early forties."

Which meant he'd be in his fifties now, thought Mansfield. "Another student? A mature student? Lecturer?"

Joanna shook her head. "I don't think so. I... I don't really know."

"Which university was this?" he asked. "What did he look like? What were the names of the other people involved?"

When she just sat there gaping, he knew he was going too fast – perhaps even asking things she couldn't remember yet. And he had to question why that was; there were many cases of cult leaders messing with people's minds, wiping out any traces of what had happened to them. Of course, there were just as many members who simply wanted to *block* things out.

"I… I can't… It's difficult to trust any of these memories, Inspector. But I do know we were all initiated into this thing. That there was a… a ceremony of sorts. I remember him dipping his finger into some kind of bowl, writing on us with liquid. Marking us. It's what made me get in touch in the first place."

"The stories," Mansfield said, "in the paper. On TV."

"The mark. The X." But it wasn't just a mark, was it? This was a brand – something done to his victims like you'd do to cattle. What she said next would affect whether he took Joanna seriously or not, in spite of the fact he was beginning to warm to her. "This was where he touched me." She rolled up the jumper's sleeve and showed him her forearm – showed him the burn.

Mansfield stood sharply and rounded the table, bending to look more closely. It was similar to the others, and looked fresh – as if it had just this minute been done. He couldn't help himself, before he knew it he was taking hold of her arm in his hands – but gently, so as not to cause her any pain. "When did…?"

Joanna looked up at him. "When… when things started to come back to me. About a day or two ago."

He shook his head. "Impossible." In the cases where it had been spotted, the reposts had said it had been done after death.

"I… I can't explain it, either. But I think it was so that he could find us, no matter what; no matter who we *became*. It's how I know that I'm next." Not branded. Pinpointed. X marking the spot, all right – the next victim. "Will… Can you help me, Inspector?"

And although he had no idea what the hell was going on then, nor whether this was even linked to the other examples, Mansfield found himself nodding. Making a promise he wished he hadn't; to be able to keep this woman safe. To stop what had happened before from happening to her.

They carried on talking, him asking questions and Joanna on the verge of being able to answer, but not quite. She was remembering as if through a fog, flashes of things that piqued his interest, but no proper clues. There were ten of them, five girls and five boys – X: the ten – picked apparently by chance as far as she understood it, and yet De Carlo insisted that they were all special... or would be.

"Some of us didn't even get on, not really. We argued," Joanna told him. "Some got along okay, some even got *together*... But that wasn't what it was all about, sex. It was always about the ten, the power of the ten." Three more to go then, Mansfield thought, if this was the mentor returning to kids he'd chosen way back when. "It was all about that, about how *we* held the power." She shrugged. "I guess everyone in their youth likes to hear that. It's one of the reasons I'm so protective of my Shaun. Oh, that's my boy – he's at university now himself. I'm so worried something bad will happen to him, I think I probably push him away sometimes."

"Have you told him about all this?" he asked her.

Joanna gave a definite shake of the head. "I wouldn't know where to start. Barely knew how to begin with you. But, well, you've just got this way about you. I feel like I'm able to open up."

Mansfield mentioned nothing about his training, about how once upon a time he'd wanted to go into psychology, counselling – until the pull of the Force took hold. Until that incident in his twenties with his folks... now gone forever. But it wasn't only that with Joanna; she wasn't merely a subject to scrutinise.

"I'm looking forward to him coming home for Christmas."

"*I'm*, you said... not *we*. The father's not around anymore?" And was there something other than professional interest, there?

Don't, he told himself... *Just don't.*

Joanna shook her head again. "I had him young, Inspector. Another... I won't say mistake, but it was because I..." Yet another shake.

Some even got together... He had to wonder whether it was because of these meetings, whether something happened at or after one of them. Whether Shaun was a product of this whole thing? A by-product of the ten? But Mansfield held his silence.

"I pretty much brought him up on my own. I mean, there have been a few guys, but never anything… He was my world, y'know? Still is, of course." There were tears in her eyes. "Broke my heart when he went off. Probably couldn't wait to get away, though." Her laugh was a melancholy one.

He wanted to say something to comfort her about it, but didn't have the words. Instead he asked again about the ten angle.

"I don't know, as I say –"

"You can only remember bits and pieces," he finished for her, familiar with it by now.

She gave a nod. "Something to do with systems of belief, how it's the most powerful of all numbers."

"In the occult, you mean?" he asked, but didn't get an answer. It was certainly used in religion if he recalled his Sunday school lessons. How many times was it in the Bible? The number of generations between Adam and Noah, for starters – and the same between Noah and Abraham for that matter. The coins, the lepers, the plagues of Egypt, the Commandments… (Thou shalt *not* kill). But the *most* powerful? "Some kind of ritual? Is that what's going on here?"

"I… I honestly don't know," she told him.

"All right," Mansfield continued, trying another tack. "You said before it was how he might be able to find you, whoever you became."

"That's just it, we all became different people – but I'm not sure whether that was our choice, just to get away. Or maybe *he* did it, created new personas for us. I… I don't believe Joanna is my real name, Inspector."

"Charles," he said, insisting that she use his.

"Charles… We might have done it to hide, but he was always going to find us because of this." She held up the exposed arm again.

It wasn't that easy to change who you were, though – in spite of what you saw on the TV, people who went into witness protection and the like. There was always a trace, if you knew where to look.

"Joanna," he started, then stopped, thinking about what she'd said about her name – but then it was the only one she'd known for years. "Look, with your permission I'd like to try something."

"What kind of something?" She bit her lip.

"I want to try and get you to remember. Put you in a more relaxed state."

"Hypnosis?"

"Nothing so extreme..." *Not yet.* "I just want to tease out some more of the details, and I think you need them out as well." Mansfield needed to know where, when, how, though... What the person who did this to them looked like. Who might be next after her, so he could protect them as well.

She seemed unsure, but nodded anyway. "Is it going to hurt?"

Mansfield laughed, an attempt put her at her ease. "Not at all."

He'd been wrong, however – very wrong. Whoever had screwed with her mind had left mental booby traps, and if he prodded with the wrong kind of enquiry 'Joanna' would writhe about in the chair, breathing heavily, on the verge or crying out at certain points. He *had* found himself apologising then, devastated that he might be hurting her.

It was during one of their breaks, while Mansfield had been calling up Troughton to arrange local accommodation for them all – although he was beginning to think maybe they should just stay right where they were until morning, until he could move Joanna safely – that everything hit the fan.

The lights had started to flicker out in the hallway, before winking off completely. Mansfield waited a few moments, waiting for the back-ups to kick in if this was just a power cut. They did, but then those started to blink as well. He popped back into the room, feeling guilty again when Joanna started.

"What's happening?" she asked him, biting her lip again, harder this time.

"I don't know... Probably nothing. Wait here, I'll go and find out."

She opened her mouth to say something, probably to ask him not to leave her alone, but she closed it, nodded. Mansfield had only taken a few steps down the corridor, was calling out to a uniformed man at the other end, when the lighting failed a final time. It seemed to him, looking back now, that something just sucked all the light out of that place like juice out of a carton.

He knew it didn't make any sense, knew also that there were dozens of officers and a security system between the front door and them, but then nothing about this whole business added up. All Mansfield knew was his hand was reaching back, curling around the grip of his Glock – which he wouldn't even have about his person if he'd been any ordinary kind of inspector in this country.

Not only that, he was in the process of drawing the weapon when something barrelled into him. Mansfield was knocked sideways and into a wall, all the wind forced out of his lungs. He slumped down, struggling to see who had attacked him – someone with extraordinary strength, that was for sure – but all he saw were shadows, a breath of wind passing by; the crackle of static. Then he lost consciousness for a moment.

The light coming back on in the corridor was what roused him, and he was suddenly being helped to his feet by the uniformed officer he'd been calling to. He was as puzzled as Mansfield about what had happened, but that didn't matter. All that mattered was:

"Joanna," said Mansfield, beckoning the policeman to come with him to the room where the interview was being conducted.

Even before he opened the door again, not bothering to look through the glass this time, he knew something had happened to her. That he'd lost her... His lead, this woman he'd promised to protect.

And there she was, hanging from – ironically – the light fitting, hanging from her scarf by the neck.

"Jesus!" exclaimed the uniformed cop, but Mansfield was pointing, tucking his gun away again and ordering him to help get her down. It wasn't too late, it *couldn't* be.

Mansfield held her body while the other man undid the knot. The inspector lowered her gently, as he'd done when examining her arm. Felt for a pulse at the neck, but was getting nothing. Then a wheeze, barely a whisper as she drifted away.

"No!" Mansfield cried, but it was already too late and in spite of his best efforts he couldn't revive her. She was gone, forever. As he stood back, breathing in and out, making up for her lack of breath, his eyes trailed down to her right hand… where the middle finger was missing.

And he mouthed the words she said to him in her final moments. The names she'd given him, remembered at last.

The names of the final two victims.

It had taken a while again, mainly because she'd given him their real names – the ones she'd known them by when they were young. That had allowed them to track the uni anyway – Bedminton – and their people were working to put the actual names to those victims who had gone before Joanna…

Given enough time, anyone could be traced.

But there had also been repercussions. Mansfield had been put on a tighter leash because of what had happened at the police station, with some even questioning whether his lines of enquiry had caused their new witness to 'commit suicide'; it was impossible to see what had actually happened in that room at her time of death, the CCTV footage not only too dark but also distorted. His own recordings were reviewed and his methods scrupulously examined. Certainly her son was out for blood, demanding to know the exact circumstances of what had occurred. If Mansfield had known himself, then he would have gladly passed that on.

What he did know was Joanna Hutchings hadn't killed *herself*. Whether it had been another one of those mental landmines that had triggered the action, or someone had been in that room and done it to her – been in that corridor with *him* – she hadn't hung herself of her own free will. How would you explain the finger? Where did that go? An inside job? Maybe that uniformed officer who had helped him? But how had he moved so quickly? He was being questioned nevertheless...

Then there was Joanna herself; the way he'd felt about letting her down, as if he owed her, *needed* to keep her safe. And failed her. Mansfield vowed there and then that wouldn't happen with the next two; vowed to stop this maniac before the killing of the Ten could be completed.

While efforts continued to link the real and fake identities and to find this so called mentor De Carlo, Mansfield started digging into the significance of the number. He discovered that not only did ten feature in those stories he'd remembered, but it was mentioned 244 times in the Bible – not least when the Holy Spirit descended upon the apostles after the Ascension of Jesus.

For Pythagorus and his followers it represented the universe – was tied in to everything – and according to Agrippa it was 'the number of all', of completeness, totality and achievement. Ten was regarded as the most perfect of numbers by some, because it stood for the created and the non-created, the beginning and the end, the power and the force, the life and the nothing. Not only that, it had been known to represent revelation and divine law. Mansfield recalled sitting back in his chair and staring at the computer screen when he read all of this, realising that there *was* power here – or at least one might be convinced there was. Power enough to kill for, if you believed strongly in it, enough to persuade a bunch of college kids to follow you, at any rate...

The more he investigated, the more he found that number everywhere – in everything. The original Roman calendar had ten months to it, but time – history itself – was broken up into increments of ten years: decades, centuries, millennia... (and this made him think about the timing of the murders; five killed ten years after they'd been marked, which made sense, but then five nineteen years afterwards? Though if you added the 1 and 9 together...)

It was there in monetary systems, in measurements and weights... Astrology (each of the thirty-six parts of the astrological Zodiacs divided into ten degrees); ten various regions of the universe corresponding to the ten psychic parts of man; conspiracy theories... Even in marking systems, 10/10 – the famous number Dudley Moore attributed to Bo Derek in the film of the same name. And binary code: just a series of 1's and 0's; in fact when you wrote 1010 you actually got the binary for ten.

Some even said that ten *meant* god. Now that probably would be worth murdering for, if you thought it would give you that kind of power.

It was as his research was drawing to a close that Troughton rang him, telling him they'd not only got the names of the next two on the kill list – but also their location.

"Location? Not *locations?*"

"They're together, sir. Married."

Some got together... "One is man, nought is woman. The union," he mumbled.

"What?"

"Doesn't matter. Tell me."

"All right, but you're never going to bloody believe it."

The whispered names, Elaine Cooper and Harry Dunn... Now Mr and Mrs Marcus Reed – Elaine hadn't even changed her first name. "Reed? As in the author?" Mansfield had asked. He'd heard of him – never picked up any of his books, but *of course* he'd heard of him. "Read Marcus Reed!" the famous advertising campaigns.

"That's the one," Troughton confirmed. "Used to write horror, some people said he was even as good as Herbert Lynch – but I didn't really rate him. Writes crime now, mostly, but with a supernatural twist. The girlfriend loves his stuff."

"Location?" he reminded the DC.

"Guy's practically a recluse, it's quite a remote –"

"*Where?*" Mansfield had snapped. They might be able to kill two birds with one stone, but then so could De Carlo. The ritual complete...

And when he'd said the name of the place, Mansfield had told Troughton to pick him up. Then the inspector had started making calls, trying to gather together men from the nearest stations to go with him at short notice – and in the holiday period...

That's how they'd ended up on this ferry, heading to a small island off the coast of Scotland – which they couldn't get in touch with because of the storm that was building.

Because of the storm that was making the vessel rock back and forth, and probably should have forced Mansfield back down below again where Troughton would be waiting with the rest of the troops. The DC had tried to get out of this duty himself, but the inspector hadn't let him off the hook that easily.

"You're the expert on this bloke," he'd said to him. "Or the closest thing we've got."

"Hardly... I just... Ah, bollocks!" had been the reply, then he'd apologised for the language. "But I'm a dead man, sir. I had some time booked off and everything, to spend with the other half."

"With a bit of luck, you can bring her back a signed copy of something – if we get to the poor sods in time."

When they eventually hit the island of Grizel, they hit it hard. It certainly felt like that as the ferry jerked forward and then back before docking. As soon as the ramps were down, though, they were off – in two cars and a van – checking maps because the satnavs and mobiles weren't working. By the time they arrived at the Reed residence, which looked like a converted old castle perched precariously on top of a hill, the rain was lashing down hard. Much worse than anything they'd encountered in Wales.

Troughton had whistled, looking up through the wipers. "Nice! And they say crime doesn't pay."

"Crime *writing* clearly does," Mansfield replied.

The gate to the property looked as if it hadn't worked even before it had been wrenched open – it was now swinging back and forth in the gale. The storm might have done that, but they proceeded with caution anyway. When they knocked on the huge front door and found that was open too, the locks smashed, it was more than enough probable cause to enter.

Guns out in front of them, and glad of the backup behind – with each officer carrying as well – Mansfield and Troughton took the lead. The inside was as old-fashioned as the exterior, with various oil paintings lining the hallway.

"Can you smell that?" asked Troughton.

Mansfield nodded. An aroma like cooked meat. They followed it into the first of two huge rooms – wall-to-wall bookcases and with a piano in the corner. These were not what drew the inspector's eye, but rather the charred remains of a body ahead of them on the velvet carpet, lying face down.

"Reed!" said Troughton. "Shit, we're too late."

As they moved forward, guns pointing first one way then another, Mansfield noted one small patch of skin on the body that wasn't burnt to a crisp. Not totally, anyway; it was burnt, just in the shape of an X – and on the small of the back. He looked then to the hands, outstretched on the ground. The thumb on the right hand was missing.

There was a noise coming from somewhere not far away, a mewling sound. Mansfield nudged Troughton, nodded for the man to join him as he checked the sound out. They tracked it down to the corner, to behind the piano, where they could see someone was hiding.

"Come out!" ordered Mansfield. "Nice and slow. Hands where we can see them."

Two shaking hands appeared, definitely male – and he realised now their mistake. Behind them on the carpet was not Marcus Reed, it was his wife Elaine. And though there were never any author photos on his books, nor did he do tours, this had to be him. Right age, definitely, and terrified.

"He's… he's here…" said the man with wide eyes and thinning blond hair. "H-He's *here!*"

Troughton looked around, swallowing hard.

Clearly it was all coming back to Reed; what had happened when he was younger, the cult of the ten and De Carlo. He was probably even feeling the unholy burn himself, as the X that had been painted on him all those years ago suddenly started to show itself. This was like the plot of one of his more outlandish novels.

"Okay… It's okay," Mansfield said. "We're going to get you out of here."

Then the lighting in the room started to flicker. Again, might have been the storm – which was even now battering the windows of that room, thunder rolling in the distance – but Mansfield doubted it. He'd seen this trick before, and he wasn't going to let that son of a bitch have this last victim.

But before they could get Reed up, get him back to the protection of the rest of the men, it was already happening. The lights failed, and the room was plunged into shadows. Then movement – muzzle flash as shots were fired, illuminating faces that were now twisted in pain. Mansfield aimed his own gun, hoping to wing the man who was somehow avoiding those blasts and tearing into their group.

Bang! Another flash and one officer was splattered in blood. *Bang!* Another, and a stocky man was being lifted and flung across the room like a ragdoll. *Bang!* the young lad who'd asked whether he was all right on the ferry, Stewart, had his mouth open as his head was twisted clean off like someone opening a jar of marmalade.

Then suddenly Troughton was moving forward, shooting bullet after bullet. There was a grunt, a gurgling noise, and he was deposited at Mansfield's feet just as the lights flickered back on, revealing the full horrors of that room. Bodies mangled, blood spilled. Mansfield looked down and saw Troughton's eyes were missing.

"Bollocks... I'm a dead man, sir!"

Shouldn't have made him come – he should be at home now with his girlfriend, relaxing on the couch, her flipping through the pages of... *Read Marcus Reed!* And he felt bad for all those times he'd barked at the young man, couldn't take it back now.

Gone, forever.

Mansfield looked across to see the target still standing there, whimpering. But no sign of anyone else. The inspector was alone, the only person who could stand between this man and his killer.

"H-Here... He's..."

"Yes, yes I know," grunted Mansfield, not meaning to snap again, but running on adrenalin. "We need to –"

The whimpering turned into a giggle, madness clearly setting in. "He's here," said the man. "Here, here, here!" He was jumping up and down.

"Look calm down, I –"

"Here," repeated the blond man. "He's *here!*" The last bit was a virtual growl, and Reed was pointing at him. At Mansfield. "You... are... here!"

Mansfield frowned, didn't have a clue what he was talking about. Reed was grinning like a lunatic; it was the kind of grin he'd seen too many times. But before he could do anything about it, like turn the gun on him, the man had clicked his fingers.

Then everything went black again.

It wasn't the kind of blackness from before, when the lights went out – this was different. This had been his own eyes closing, shutting out the light that was in the room.

Maybe someone had knocked him out, crept up behind him and whacked him on the back of the head, just like Linda Nilsson (no, Hannah Bridgewater); except he hadn't felt any pain. It had been more like falling asleep when you couldn't remember dropping off.

Some kind of suggestion. The snapping of the fingers...

And now, he was drifting towards consciousness again. Aware

of things – aware of how dark it still was. How cold; just like Joanna's hand (even colder now). He was lying flat, as far as he could tell. Inside something, some kind of container. His first thought was a coffin… Had that thing which had taken out his men attacked him too, not quite killed him but enough to look like he was dead? Was this the Poe effect? Had he been buried alive, or placed in one of those drawers in the morgue he'd visited so many times himself?

He couldn't move… No, that wasn't strictly true. Mansfield could move his head, a little. It was growing lighter and he realised it was simply because his eyes were opening wider – and also that he was rising. Tilting, the container forcing him upright. Now he was standing rooted – frozen – to the spot. Blinking away the blurriness, he could see that he was in the second room – the one he hadn't made it to.

In front of him arranged in the shape of an 'X' were jars filled with clear fluid. Floating in the liquid were the digits that had been taken from the nine victims… no, ten now he counted. He was too late.

"Ah, you're awake! I've been waiting patiently – but then, as you've probably gathered, I'm quite a patient man." The voice from behind him; the person who had tipped the 'coffin'. It was different, less excited than before, but definitely the man he'd taken for Reed – who now stepped in front of him. "I've waited so long, what was another couple of days?"

Days? thought Mansfield? But he could hear the thunder outside, see flashes of lightning through the windows. The storm still raging outside, still cutting off this tiny island from the world.

As if reading his mind the man waved a hand. "It knows, you see. The world, the universe. Knows what's coming. What's about to happen… And this place, a nexus, a crossroads. That's why I chose it. I hope you didn't mind me putting you on ice." He gave a little chuckle. "But I needed you here for the endgame."

Mansfield experimentally looked down, though it pained him

to do so. His naked body was covered in tubes, which ran in and out of him, filled with more liquid – this time blue.

"Very experimental stuff. It's a similar procedure to dialysis – allows me to control your temperature. You've been kept on the brink since you arrived and now I'm allowing you to wake up... You'd know all about it if you'd ever picked up Marcus Reed's novel, *The Cooler.*" He laughed again. "You're confused, I can understand that – and the least I can do is clear that up, while we still have time."

Mansfield gritted his teeth, attempted to speak. "Y-You... w-work f-for De... De Carlo," he managed.

"Oh my dear Inspector, haven't you put it together yet?" He touched his chest. "I *am* De Carlo! That's what I called myself back then, anyway. Just my little joke... De C. Dec? No?"

"B-But..."

The man stroked his own face. "It's all part of the power. Better than a facelift, isn't it? Hey presto, from grey back to blond again. It's where this comes from, too." He moved then, across the room and back again, so quickly Mansfield had trouble following him. "And this." The man was gone again, this time into the adjoining room, and he returned holding the piano above his head. Mansfield's jaw was hanging open. "Not bad for a sixty year old, eh?" He returned the instrument and was back in a flash. "There are other benefits, of course." Now he pointed up at the lights, made them flicker, then die. Seconds later it was light again. "Works on CCTV cameras as well... The power."

"H-Harry D-Dunn... You've killed him, then."

De Carlo shook his head. "No, not yet. Not until midnight. As I said, I'm a patient man and this has been unfolding a long time. The research, then the gathering of the ten. The sacrifices."

"M-Murders," Mansfield corrected. Lives snuffed out, gone forever.

He sneered then. "Every single one agreed. Gave themselves willingly to be part of something bigger."

"M-Mind c-control," said the inspector through chattering

teeth.

"Not control; a necessity to create new lives, new identities. Until it was time."

"F-For the r-rituals."

De Carlo's face soured. "For the *ceremony.* The *sacrament.* In they end they all remembered – they needed to. Though some had changed their minds, it was too late. They bore the mark." He made an invisible cross in the air in front of him. "It was harder to complete the task to begin with, naturally – so I used poison, a gun. The way it was carried never really mattered, not as much as the taking of the fingers; the parts of our bodies that let us touch, feel... *do.* And at the same time I was bringing us all together again, I was growing stronger. Faster. Younger."

"C-Crazy," Mansfield spluttered. Not even he was sure whether he meant De Carlo or what he was hearing, seeing. More hypnosis, more mind control – it had to be, only this time performed on him.

"On the contrary, it all makes perfect sense. There have been attempts going back centuries, millennia even. Some more recent grabs for the grand title, for the crown: a shapeshifter who thought he was a wolf; the Order of the Shadows... I have to admit, I stole a bit of their act for some of my performances. Oh, and one you might be familiar with, a man who could absorb twins' souls. I think you people called him The Gemini."

Now that name Mansfield did know. He'd read the files on that particular killer, read the deluded man's diary entries as well; they were discovered after the fire in Norchester. They were just as insane as De Carlo's beliefs... or whatever the hell his name was, and his attempts to turn himself into something that could never be. Power struggles far beyond mob bosses for control of a city...

"None of which concerns us, though, because I got there in the end."

It was Mansfield's turn to laugh. "A... A god."

The blond man's brow furrowed. "A god? You think that is

what's happening here? What I will become? No, no, no. The ten, the perfect entity – that is the god. I will be..." He held up his two first fingers and brought them together. "Something *more* – or that's the theory." He smiled. "So, what do you think of my little scheme, Inspector?"

Mansfield couldn't find the words.

De Carlo shook his head. "Ah well, not to worry. Like my 'darling wife', you have already given me the thumbs up." He bent and picked up one of the jars, showing it to Mansfield.

His darling...

"You... so you're –"

"Read Reed!" He gave a bow. "I came up with that one actually – the marketing and publicity people love me. It's so easy to manipulate the press, don't you find?" Not Kendrick then, but *him* all along; controlling *everything* (he'll wish he'd never been born...). "Though Reed was never, ever Harry Dunn. That was just another trail of breadcrumbs I left so the real Harry would find his way to me. What can I say, I have friends in high places."

"He's here!" The insane man he was there to protect pointing at him. *"You... are... here!"*

"Go on, join the dots Harry. *Remember.*"

Mansfield looked from the thumb in the jar, down to where his left thumb should have been. Saw also the 'X' there emerging on the back of his hand.

And then it all came flooding back to him.

University, studying psychology – but not Bedminton, it couldn't have been... Could it? Young, away from home and... just that little bit lost. Needing some kind of mentor and answering that ad in the back of the uni newspaper, same as the others. Wanting to be part of... of something more. Responding to this man who had all the answers, who taught them about the power of the ten and what could be achieved. Falling in love (*some of us got together*) with Joanna, who had been Nancy back then (and, no... hadn't she been... there had been a baby; a son... *his* son, for the love of...). And he had agreed to it willingly, hadn't he?

Let the mark be placed on him, only to forget all about it until it appeared again nineteen years later... Leaving everything he'd ever known behind, becoming someone else, with a different path – though actually named after the place he grew up in. With parents that hadn't really existed, who'd been killed by a random nutter (oh Christ, his mother, his father... they were still alive!) and spun him off into the police force. All engineered, all plotted as precisely as one of Marcus Reed's novels and just as mad.

Steering him towards the SCI, towards this particular investigation (had this man even been behind the offer?). Waiting, waiting...

What's another couple of days? And if he was missed, if they'd sent more police to the island in the meantime, then they would be just as dead as the men he'd come here with. Stood no chance against someone with the power of the... of the nine. Not complete.

Not dead. Not yet.

Not done yet, Harry Dunn...

"That's it, I can see the memories in your eyes." De Carlo leaned back. "And so we can begin." He'd already placed Mansfield's – no, not his real name – thumb back down with the others and now the blond man was flipping a switch on the box the tubes were threading into. Turning down the temperature just so, freezing him, freezing his very blood. "The other sacraments... Well, it was always going to *end* with fire and ice," De Carlo told him, holding up another finger with one hand and creating a nought with the finger and thumb of his other. "The two opposites."

The thunder was growing louder outside, the lightning striking the castle – like something out of an old Universal movie. But it wasn't Frankenstein's monster that would be created this time but something else – if this man was correct.

"Almost time," he said, nodding to himself. "Almost midnight. The start of a brand new year. A brand new *era*, Harry."

And as he slowly froze, the man who thought he'd been

Inspector Charles Mansfield – who had lived that life for so long – realised the date of the new year, and what you got when you added up the numbers 2017.

De Carlo strolled over to a table on his right, pouring himself a generous amount of what was probably quite expensive whiskey. He held up the glass for a toast, as the life ebbed out of his final victim. His last volunteer, the one who would complete the sacrament.

"Well, here's to it then. Here's to the power…" He paused. Lightning flashed a final time and was it Mansfield's… Harry's imagination or did the man's eyes change colour then?

"Here's to the power of Ten. The power of *The Ten*," was the last thing he heard.

Before everything went black again… one last time.

The life, the light gone now…

Forever.

Twisted Limerick 1

Ramsey Campbell

I wonder if Harry cried "Oi!
It was made out of lentils and soy.
And it's no kind of joke
To compose it from folk.
It's a concept that brings me no joy."

We Know By the Tenth Day Whether They Live Or Die

Simon Clark

Day One

The infestation had struck other parts of the world. You know the kind of places where you expect this kind of thing to happen: hot tropical swamps where cholera, typhoid, or some hideous flesh-eating disease erupts, slaughtering thousands. Not here, though. Not the placid British Isles with its harmless wildlife and cool climate that seems such a poor environment for any plague bug or virulent parasite to survive, never mind spread.

The infestation did arrive, however. A loathsome, stomach-churning infestation that seemed too incredible to believe in at first. But believe we did, eventually. In fact, we not only accepted the existence of those vile creatures with their shining, iridescent skins, we even accommodated them. And when they latched onto someone we loved we kept the entire thing secret. We quietly waited out the ten days in the hope that whoever had become a victim of the Snake would successfully separate from the parasite and return to us, if not completely unscathed, at least alive and relatively undamaged.

On that first day – Day One – my wife went out into the garden where steps led down to a small underground cell or chamber that had served variously as wine cellar, air raid shelter and tool shed over the last hundred years or so.

My wife, June, a thirty-nine year old schoolteacher, had paused by the kitchen table where I sat with a tablet, trawling the internet in the hope of finding a sensibly-priced holiday cottage in Snowdonia. The spring morning was warm after a heavy shower.

I remember I'd burnt my mouth because I'd been too quick to sip the coffee.

"Bloody, damn it," I chuntered, then sucked my top lip. "How about this one? Two bedrooms. Snowdon views. Two hundred and fifty a week? Hmm, good size television."

She frowned. "We're planning to do more than watch telly, aren't we?"

"Wi-fi, DVD, parking space. It's got the lot."

"Show me when I get back. I want to check the folding chairs are still fit for purpose. See you in a minute."

With that she went out to the garden cellar. Of course, she didn't see me in a minute. The next time I saw her she'd been taken by the Snake.

Day Two

The rest of Day One became a blur after I'd discovered June and the Snake. I have only hazy, unfocussed memories of the hours that followed: of phoning my parents asking – no, if I'm being honest about this – demanding that they collect my two sons from school and keeping them at their house until I collected them, which, whatever the outcome, would be at least ten days away. I didn't give my parents an explanation. They didn't ask for one, either, perhaps sensing marital crisis.

I'd seen news about the Snake infestation in the tropics. Yet nothing prepares you for the emotional impact of seeing one of the monsters in real life – nor the absolute shock of realising that the person you love has been taken. There's no violence, no sudden movements (or so I've learnt); the process happens slowly: smoothly in a way you'd associate with how a big, cold-blooded serpent would move. Of course, I never saw June actually being caught. By the time I'd entered the garden cellar, the attack, if that's the correct word, had already taken place.

Day Two was when I came to my senses after the shock of discovering them. I found myself sitting on the cellar steps, gazing into that cold subterranean vault. There, in the corner, behind the lawnmower, the old upright vacuum cleaner, and boxes of old toys, were the pair of them, cuddled against where two walls met.

That's when I stepped outside myself. No emotion touched me. Simply, I felt cold – completely detached from a sight that had shocked me so much that I'd spent the first night there in a semi-conscious state, not eating, not drinking, not even feeling the need to go pee.

This, hereafter, is what I wrote – plain, direct, roughly jotted down by the light of a single lightbulb hanging from the ceiling – a light fitting, *spider-webbed and shouting with incandescent lips* (as Dylan Thomas might have described, or has the shock of June's tragedy left me a wee bit unbalanced?). So, this is my there-and-then description of the worst thing I've ever seen.

June sits; her back to the wall. She sleeps. Breathing deeply. Eyelids closed. Her face seems discoloured, like she's been blushing, and though the pinkness of the blush has gone it leaves blotchy darkness. The Snake is almost as long as her, and drapes over her legs that are outstretched in front of her as she sits. The Snake is half as thick as her waist. Has a flattened face, a straight line for a mouth, small eyes that resemble chips of glass that glitter. The eyes don't move. Nor does it blink. Does the creature possess eyelids? I cannot tell. They are almost face-to-face; six inches of air separate the eyes. I don't know why they called this creature 'Snake' because it's more lizard. A long row of stumpy limbs run down either side of its body (no fingers, no claws); they cling onto June. They hold her tight. They won't let go.

I don't touch the Snake.

No, and I don't touch June, either.

This is the worst thing that's ever happened to me.

•

Day Three

June's first husband, Mark, dropped by. He must have rung the house doorbell before noticing that the entrance to the garden cellar was open. He found the three of us – me sitting at the bottom of the stairs, watching; June and the Snake in the corner.

Sleep deprivation and dehydration meant that I couldn't make sense of what Mark said or did for a while. When my head cleared I realised he was holding a glass of water to my lips, telling me to drink, then saying: "I came to tell you that Katy would be coming back from university this week. She wanted to visit you."

These words hit me like a thrown brick. "No!" I shook my head, spraying out a mouthful of water as I shouted. "She can't see her mother like this!"

"I know, I know... I'll tell Katy that both of you are away."

"No phoning, either."

Mark stared at the pair in the corner – their clinch reminded me of when frogs mate, the male holding onto the female for days.

"Tom," he said, "when did you find them like this?"

"Yesterday."

Mark shuddered. "Then there are eight days left until you know how it's going to go."

That seemed such a cold way of putting an inescapable truth.

Day Four

Mark wanted to report the Snake to the police.

I had other ideas. "No. We're keeping this secret."

"You can't leave June here, wrapped up with this... *thing!*" He shone a torch on my wife and the reptile; his eyes stretched wide with shock. "Look how it's holding her. We don't know if it's feeding on her, or – or laying eggs inside her body."

I turned away, not wanting to see my wife being held by the creature in such a brilliant, detail-revealing light. June still slept. Neither she nor the creature had moved. They simply seemed to be sleeping there in the corner. June's T-shirt and jeans bore grimy patches now. In fact, everywhere in that cellar seemed to have acquired a film of dirt. Walls, shelves, boxes appeared newly grubby. Even the lightbulb became dimmer as if smeared with some muddy substance.

Mark said, "The walls where they're sitting..." His expression was one of disgust. "The brickwork's painted white, but the walls are turning black. Is it mold?"

I shrugged. I didn't know what caused the darkening. The walls were blacker and blacker by the hour. Absolute black nearest the pair. Bible black.

"Please, Tom, call the police."

"No. You've seen what happens to women when one of those things latches onto them. If they're forced apart the woman dies of shock."

"What if it's feeding on her, or laying eggs?" He'd said this before. The disgusting notion obsessed him.

"That's never happened."

"As far as we know. Phone the police, Tom."

I shook my head. "We can't tell anyone about June. You know what'll happen to her if you do."

He shone the torch into June's face. My wife's nose and cheeks had become dull. All the shine had gone. The Snake was different. Its skin was brighter than before – the scales becoming glossy, smooth, iridescent – the same multicolour rainbow effect engine oil has on a puddle of water. In other circumstances I might have said that its skin was beautiful.

"I hope she doesn't wake up," Mark stated. "At least not until it's over."

Whenever Mark stood near June I always pictured them when they were man and wife. And that mind-picture always involved them being naked together. Mark pushing his cock into her. In my imagination the sex is all very visible and slippery. Wet-looking; lots of blissful sighs and moaning. Try as I might, I can't stop myself picturing my wife coupling with Mark. Peculiar; almost as if I'm punishing myself, but I've nothing to feel guilty about regarding June and her ex. Their marriage was over before I even met her.

After a while, I sat down on the cellar step. Mark joined me. He stared at his ex-wife. I closed my eyes. Mental images of his thick fingers kneading her breasts filled my head.

Mark said, "I know what you're thinking."

"Oh?"

"It's awful, but we'll get through this. June will be okay again. It just takes ten days, then the Snake will go."

"When they part, some women die."

"June's strong."

We sat without talking for a long time.

Mark then said, "Have you finished writing the Dylan Thomas book?"

The Snake gripped my wife with its stubby little arms. This wasn't the time for small-talk. I didn't answer his question.

Mark patted my knee. "I'm sure it will be a good book. You'll make money, and you and June can have a long holiday."

My blood went cold. "I can't see a time when life will ever get back to normal."

"Tom, I know a doctor. We could bring her here?"

"No. Nobody must know. If people find out, they'll treat her like she's a leper. And that's not just short-term, that'll be for the rest of her life."

Day Five

Mark shook me gently by the shoulder.

"Did you hear what I said?" he asked.

Those big grey eyes of his fixed on mine. He was clearly worried.

"What?" For a moment I didn't realise I was still in the cellar.

Mark's expression of worry became even more obvious. "Tom, you've hardly left the cellar in days. Your skin's like ice. You need to warm up."

"I'm alright. I'm staying here with June."

"You can't sit on that step for another five days."

"I'm not leaving her."

"Get a hot bath and something to eat."

I shook my head: the pair in the corner – Snake and June –

that's what I focussed on. Nothing else mattered. I'd pledged to keep a vigil until the tenth day. I tried to speak clearly but I knew I was mumbling.

"I'm going to wait it out, Mark. You can't stop me."

"You're not looking well. It's damp and it's cold."

"Staying." I grunted. "Just in case she…" I couldn't push the last words out through my lips.

"Tom. If you don't take a break I'll phone for an ambulance." He glared at me now. "Not for June – for you."

"You wouldn't."

"Just you try me."

"I can't leave her alone with that thing."

"Don't worry." His voice became kind again. "I'll stay with her." He squeezed my forearm – a gesture of such affection that tears came into my eyes. "A bath, hot food: that's what you need."

Too choked-up to reply, I managed to stand up. My legs were dead after sitting on the cellar step for so long.

"Don't worry, Tom," he said. "I'll be here."

I thudded unsteadily up the steps.

"Call me if there's any change." I told him before heading for the house. "Even if it's the slightest thing. Okay?"

I stepped out into the daylight. Its sheer intensity blinded me.

Thirty minutes later, I'd dunked myself in hot bathwater, drank coffee, scalding my mouth and throat and hardly noticed the pain. My meal consisted of what I could pick out of the fridge – so I quickly chomped down lettuce leaves, tomato, cheese, cold roast chicken, yoghurt, a slice of Bavarian smoked ham, then more coffee, searingly hot.

The Snake had captured the woman I loved. I hadn't been able to prevent the attack, nor could I free her now. That was the situation, which I couldn't undo or even modify. The Snake would hold her in its stubby arms for ten days. If I tried to kill the Snake or forcibly pull them apart then June would die. There had been enough tragic incidents in the last few months to prove that to be the case, so any intervention was a no-no.

I sat there at the kitchen table with a coffee in my hands and I understood that as well as cementing itself to my wife of twelve years, the creature had also created a private world for me to live in. Yes, a peculiar notion. However, as I looked around the kitchen, and then out through the window at the trees, I realised that I seemed to inhabit a new world that was near-identical to the one I'd lived in before June's encounter. The dimensions and sizes of trees, walls, kitchen fittings and so on all seemed ever-so slightly changed. The colours were duller. Of course, shock had done this to me. I understood that. Yet the world I occupied was a place I couldn't trust. Look at what had been inflicted on June. My surroundings, somehow, had become threatening. The windows seemed to be on the verge of bursting inwards to gouge my face with broken glass. Is this a symptom of paranoia? Had the experience damaged me psychologically?

The next thing I knew I had the tablet in my hands, searching for accounts written by friends and family of people who'd been taken by the Snake. For the next hour I read #Snakecapture Tweets. I scoured websites, and I watched films on YouTube of unconscious women in the grip of that disgusting reptile.

Day Six

Once again, Mark persuaded me to take a break from watching over June. After an hour nibbling sandwiches, while poring over websites, I made a coffee for Mark.

My first words to him on my return were: "Any change? Anything different?"

He shook his head as he took the coffee from me. "Cheers."

"Listen. I've been checking up on this…" I couldn't bring myself to say 'Snake' – even to think the word made me queasy. "Over seventy percent of people survive."

Mark nodded firmly. "June'll make it. Trust me."

"But what will she be like afterwards? Websites say that

women are never the same again. And the victims are always women, never men."

"She won't be damaged goods, Tom."

"Survivors of this are affected mentally. Lots shut themselves up at home and never go out."

"June won't be like that."

"How can you be sure? You don't know her like I do!"

He gave me a look, the one that said clearly that he did know the woman as well as I did. After all, he'd been married to her for three years. That's over a thousand nights sleeping in the same bed together. A lot of intimacy.

"Tom," he said in a gentle voice. "We'll help her through whatever comes afterwards."

"What if the neighbours find out? They'll shun her! Because that's what happens. I've been reading Tweets from hundreds of women saying that even their own families turn their backs on them."

"Calm down."

"That's easy for you to say. You go back home after all this is over!"

"I'll help you both. Trust me."

"How can she trust you? You pissed off after she'd given birth to Katy!"

"Tom –"

"You know something, it's like people smell Snake on their victims. June's friends will instinctively know what's happened. They'll have nothing to do with her. Okay, they can't help themselves! But they won't be able to stomach being anywhere near her."

"Stop shouting at me, Tom. I'm doing my best to –"

"Aw, piss off! Go on, get out of my sight!"

I knocked the coffee out of his hand, then shoved him up the cellar steps.

I yelled, "Get out! We don't need you!"

"Tom –"

"Shut up!"

"Tom, stop this."

"Go home!"

"Tom! She's waking up!"

We both rushed back into the cellar room. There in the corner a change had begun to take place. The Snake clung to June with its stumpy limbs. Its rainbow skin flushed – coruscated: bands of red, green, blue, orange and yellow flowed across its flesh: a multi-coloured blushing effect. June and the creature were face-to-face, perhaps ten inches apart.

June's eyes were open. They widened in horror. Straight away, she tried to pull back, her face turning to a mask of revulsion.

"June," I shouted. "Can you hear me?"

She didn't say anything, or even give any indication she'd heard. Her frightened eyes had locked onto the flat reptile face in front of her. She managed to raise one hand to try and shove the ugly thing away.

Mark gasped. "What will happen if she breaks free?"

June pushed at that face just in front of hers. The shoves were initially powerful ones. Yet they quickly faded in strength until she only patted the scaled hide. The expression of fear receded. Her eyelids became heavy, as if she felt drowsy.

She stared at the glittering scales. "Shiny," she murmured. "So shiny."

She now stroked the Snake's body with the palm of her hand. I watched as her hand moved gently across the gleaming scales as if she gently stroked a kitten.

"So shiny," she whispered again, then her eyelids slowly closed once more.

I took a step closer, watching her face closely; she was unconscious.

Mark whispered: "It's drugged her. The thing must secrete a chemical that's sent her back to sleep."

We sat down, side-by-side, on the cellar steps. We could do nothing other than continue our vigil. Just as I couldn't stop myself picturing Mark and June having sex, now I began to imagine what would happen on Day Ten. There was no evidence that the Snake laid eggs in the women they took, yet I was assaulted by vivid images of women shrieking in panic as torrents of tiny, wet, wriggling snakes gushed from every orifice of their bodies.

Day Seven

Exhaustion gripped me. Mark opened up a deckchair for me to rest in as I maintained my vigil there in the chilly cellar, with my wife and the monster in the corner. Did the cold affect her, or (and it was a sickening thought) did the Snake keep her warm, pressed up tight against her like that?

A few hours later, I returned to the step and Mark took my place in the deckchair.

Soon Mark fell asleep, his face covered by a blanket, so only the top of his head poked out. A spider ran through his hair as he dozed, spinning webs, giving him flecks of white in those thick, black curls of his.

June and the Snake were still. From time to time, I checked if she was still breathing. Even so, I never touched her or the creature. Rumours abounded on the internet that to even lay the lightest of fingers on a captive of a Snake would result in the person dying of shock.

My biography, *Dylan Thomas – The Film Years*, absorbed me for the rest of the day. I only planned to re-read a couple of chapters I'd written; those words, however, became my fortress, protecting me from reality. I started working on a chapter about Thomas scripting a wartime propaganda film called *Deeper than the Submarine Swims*. Eagerly, I entered the world of Britain in 1945, picturing the Welsh poet sitting in a pub where, fuelled by beer and cigarettes, he wrote his script. Often work is an escape from our troubles. Dylan Thomas' intense concentration as he laboured over a story of hunted submariners arguably made him forget violent arguments with his wife, Caitlin, and the landlord's demands for unpaid rent.

For the first time in days I forgot about the thing in the corner.

Day Eight

Most of the time Mark and I sat in silence. A brooding, gloomy silence at that.

We'd not spoken for hours when an object exploded into the cellar. A screeching, fast-moving object that hurtled around the room.

"Get it out!" Mark shouted.

The intruder was a magpie. We'd left the cellar door open for fresh air and the bird had invaded that silent place that could have become a tomb for my future happiness. We waved our arms as the big black and white bird thrashed its wings, rocketing from one side of the cellar to the other.

"Don't let it touch June," I told him; although how he could realistically prevent such a thing I don't know.

We shouted at the magpie, while trying to herd the fluttering beast back to the staircase. At last, after leaving a black feather as souvenir of its visit, the bird flew up the steps, back to the outside world.

The intrusion left us agitated. We paced the floor (keeping our distance from the two in the vile clinch), while suddenly talking to one another in a brittle way.

"Magpies are vermin," I snapped. "They eat dead rats. There could be all kinds of bacteria sprayed over the place."

"It's shit on the deckchair." Mark angrily ran his fingers through his hair. He didn't attempt to clear away the blob of white from the canvas.

Of course, the subject changed to what preoccupied our minds.

"When they separate, where will that go?" Mark jabbed his finger in the direction of the Snake.

"More's to the point, where do they come from?" I scratched

my face, feeling abrasive stubble. I hadn't shaved since all this started. "After all, nobody knew that these bastards even existed until a couple of years ago."

"The sea, that's where scientists think they came from."

"Now some're saying an earthquake in Burma released them from caves, and they're swimming through the sea, spreading all over the world."

We paced, debated, not fully listening to what the other said. The magpie's shocking intrusion had left us cranky.

Mark still ran his fingers through his hair. "They latch onto women. It's like these things are giant leeches."

"I watched films on YouTube after they detach themselves. They just crawl away and vanish. If they're caught they soon melt down to a pool of... of snotty slime. You know? Like if you put salt on a slug. They liquefy."

"Why do they fix themselves to women? Is it laying eggs? Feeding?"

I stopped pacing, my blood running cold. "The day after tomorrow, Mark: it's Day Ten. Then we'll know if June lives or dies."

The words came out of me in a rush. That's when the dread hit home again. I sank down to sit on one of the cellar steps, staring at June and wondered if this time next week there'd be a funeral.

Day Nine

I don't know about anyone else but I find that unusual events attract additional, and unexpected, situations. Tragedies are accompanied by novel accessories.

When my mother underwent surgery on Christmas Eve last year I waited in the hospital canteen for her to come out of theatre. All around me were nurses wearing Christmas novelty fancy dress, including elf outfits even down to plastic pointed ears. I could only imagine the shock of a patient waking after a general anaesthetic to see a lifelike elf telling them that everything is fine and not to worry.

Just to confirm my hypothesis, regarding the Law of Sod, in the cellar, already nightmarish events took another even more dangerously bizarre twist.

Mark and I had fallen asleep. He dozed in the deckchair. I was dead to the world on a row of boxes that I'd put together to form a bunk, topped with an inflated lilo. We must both have been exhausted. That's the only explanation I can give for why we slept through as much as we did.

We woke to find the room already filling with water, and more of the stuff pouring down the cellar steps.

Mark sloshed his way to the steps and rushed up them to see what was happening. "It's raining cats and dogs up here! Your bloody drains are blocked!"

I clambered off my bunk to discover that the water came up to my knees. June and the Snake occupied the corner of the room, still motionless, both apparently asleep (that is if a reptile does actually sleep).

"Clear the drains," I shouted up at Mark. "And close the door."

"I can't! The force of the water's too much. It's a river out here. Besides, is there any point, is this thing really waterproof?"

He was right – the door was old and wooden and never meant to be airtight – but we had to do *something*, so I went to help him in any case. The staircase opened into a small hut on the back lawn. There was a door that could be locked. Now floodwater poured through. Mark tried to pull the door shut from the outside. I helped him, pushing as hard as I could from the other side.

"This is ridiculous," Mark panted. "Even if we succeed we'll never get the door open again and you'll be stuck in there. You'll drown! What good will you be to June then?"

In frustration, we abandoned the effort. "Clear the grates!" I directed instead.

"All of them?" he shouted in disbelief. "The ones in the street must be choked, too! All the run-off's pouring into your garden."

A loud pop came from behind me; instantly, the cellar lightbulb died.

"The water's got into the electrics." I let go of the door, which I'd only been able to budge by a centimetre anyway.

"The cellar's going to flood." Tom's eyes were big and scared looking. "June will drown."

"We can't touch her."

"We've got to."

"If she separates from that thing now the shock will kill her."

"You can't leave her to drown."

Day Ten was still two days away. Separation from that parasite worm of a thing and its human captive had to occur naturally. But what could I do? Watch June as water rose up over her face? Or take a chance with –

Mark grabbed my arm, "What are you going to do?"

"I don't know, but I can't just leave her alone down there."

"You're her husband, Tom. This has to be your call."

I splashed down the waterfall that now gushed over the steps. Half way, I missed my footing and slipped all the way down; a stab of pain shot through my foot. I opened my mouth to yell, but already I'd hit the pool, which was almost a metre deep. Cold water, as fast as a boxer's fist, rammed against my teeth before filling my throat. I struggled to my feet, coughing. Mark slammed into my back, almost knocking me over.

I remember swearing at him as I regained my balance. After that, I blundered through the dark to the shelves where I'd left the torches. After groping amongst hammers, screwdrivers, bits of string, I found a torch and hit the switch.

"My God!" cried Mark.

Because the light revealed the cellar had become an underground swimming pool. Cardboard boxes, pieces of wood, tennis balls, and old newspapers I kept for the rare times I decorated, floated in that brown swill.

"Put the torch on June," Mark shouted. "Shine the light on

her!"

The blaze of silver revealed the pair in the corner. June still sat with her back to the wall. The Snake remained in the same place. Neither reacted to the influx. Both were in a comatose state. The Snake's eyes were open (then they never closed, anyway; perhaps the creature really didn't have eyelids?). June's eyes were shut, however. The water level had reached her chin.

Mark punched my arm. "Tom, you've got to get her out of here."

"No!"

"She'll drown."

"If they separate now she'll die."

"She'll die anyway."

"Don't you see? If she drowns it won't by my fault. But if I free her?" My entire body shook – fear not the cold water. "I can't be the one who causes her death. I won't have that on my conscience."

Mark could have pushed by me and tried to pull the reptile's limbs away that held my wife. He didn't.

Instead, he looked me right in the eye. "This is your decision, Tom. I won't do anything without your say-so."

"We'll wait. Maybe the water won't rise any higher."

The level did rise. As it did so, a bubble, resembling a giant soap bubble emerged from the Snake's mouth, growing larger and larger. We watched as that shining sphere pressed against June's face. A moment later its surface tension seemed to give and suddenly the bubble enclosed June's head.

Surely the bubble will burst. The thought repeated over and over in my head. The bubble didn't pop. The iridescent sphere, inflated with air, formed a protective shell around June's head, something like a space helmet from a cartoon strip.

She was still breathing as the water level rose and rose until I could see her face no more.

We sat at the top of the cellar steps, gazing down into the murky liquid that filled the staircase to the halfway mark. June was down there. She and *it*, submerged. The phrase that haunted me?

Watery tomb.

Day Ten

Darkness fell at the end of Day Ten. The Snake erupted from the waters that filled the lower part of the staircase. Smoothly, that damned thing ascended the steps with anaconda grace (as Dylan Thomas might have put penned; yes, a strange observation on my part – funny how segments of our mind can be so detached from even the most horrendous of situations). Mark and I scrambled up from the top step, where we'd been sitting, and moved out onto the lawn before the Snake emerged. The creature's short, thick limbs were lying flush against its body. Moving in a smooth, serpent way, gliding through the garden, the monstrosity eventually disappeared into the night.

"They've separated." Mark's statement was unnecessary, but perhaps the words had to be said for the truth to register.

We rushed down the staircase. Flood levels had dropped, leaving a metre thick space between the surface of the water and the cellar roof.

I shone the torch across the room. June stood in the corner, her eyes open, staring directly at me. The bubble that had enclosed her head had gone. A moment later she fainted with a sigh and sank beneath the surface of the water.

Ten Months Later

Being immersed in the flooded cellar, being in the embrace of the Snake for ten days; June emerged from that nightmarish time without a mark on her body, or the stain of neurosis on her mind. Life resumed its regular rhythm of old. My Dylan Thomas biography appeared to a fanfare of glorious reviews. Happy days.

By mutual agreement, June and I never discuss what happened in the cellar. Mark never mentions it on the rare occasions he drops by. He always keeps his distance from June, as if the prospect of being within touching distance of her repels him. Our two boys, family, friends and neighbours don't know about the Snake taking possession of June. That Snake is gone and we have the rest of our lives to live.

Yes, indeed, happy days. Until, that is, last night, when we lay in bed side-by-side. June was fast asleep on her back. I rested my hand on her bare stomach. Something as firm as a muscle seemed to squirm beneath her skin, and as I lay in the gloom her tongue slid out of her mouth to stand upright in the air. The pink flesh continued to slip out between her lips until its tip was ten inches above her mouth; there the tongue swayed slightly in the gloom – and I will swear until my dying day that I saw a pair of tiny, glittering eyes embedded amongst the taste buds. The eyes were staring at me.

Twisted Limerick 2

Ramsey Campbell

Will you look what they've done to the Shire!
This new breed of hobbits is dire.
Now we're back from the wars
We must gird up our drawers
And pull the place out of the mire.

One Little Mouth To Kiss You Goodnight

Lynda E. Rucker

1

This is a story about the way the world came to an end, or perhaps how it began again. No one is really certain whether either or both has happened; after all, it has never been done before, or maybe it has, many times, but if so, we would not know about it, would we?

2

Birdie is running through the woods. The day is thick and damp and so hot she can't breathe. She's soaking wet like she's at the bottom of a swimming pool, but the woods around her are dry as her dead grandmother's bones.

Called me a boy. Told them I was a bird.

Her grandmother had known what she was, even before Birdie herself knew. *You're my little girl.* Touching Birdie's skinny lanky limbs. *Just like a bird.* Birdie's mother would say, she's confused, she's mixed you up with your sister, Donna, but she hadn't, she never did. Birdie's grandmother always knew exactly who she was.

But she'd been dead forever. Her grandmother, that is, not Birdie. Birdie's going to live until the sun dies and then she's going to go on living. She'll be the only creature left. No light. No air. No warmth. Maybe she won't be able to walk. Maybe she'll just lie on the surface of the dead earth and move her limbs about. Maybe she'll fly.

Spiderwebs are laced branch to branch, and their sticky remnants cling to her long hair and trail behind her like magic.

They can do magic. They can show me magic.

When she first sees the sign up ahead, she thinks it isn't real, but it is. It's made from weather-beaten old boards nailed across an ancient tree, has to be ancient because its trunk is so wide, but the sign itself is new, or new-ish, white paint spattered across crumbling boards announcing:

The Tetractys.

It must be them.

Birdie knows she has come home.

3

Pythagoras uncovered the secrets of the universe: numbers, and music. Well over two thousand years ago, he and his followers knew as much if not more than we do now about what is sacred and what is true. Also central to Pythagoreans was the tetractys of the decad, or the ten-pointed triangle: rows of one, two, three, and four points, divinity enfolded within the equilateral triangle. The tenth point is the point of creation and destruction. One begats the other, again and again, in an endless cycle of death and rebirth.

4

Later, they tell her she collapsed there. They tell her, these women who surround her, with their secret knowledge and their secret power and their secret ways. They tell her she is ill, and it is just like when she had a bad fever once, when she was little and her grandmother was still alive. The days melt into one another until one comes when she is able to sit up a little and talk.

They do not know her name or anything about her, but they know that if someone comes to them, that someone does not wish to be returned to wherever they came from. So they have not sent her away. They have taken care of her and given her foul-tasting things to drink which they say is medicine. She imagines they must be made from healing herbs.

The first person she sees when she wakes up – really wakes up as opposed to fitful feverish delirium awakenings – is a woman with hair as black as her own, but otherwise she looks very different from Birdie. For starters, Birdie's just sixteen and this woman must be at least sixty. Where Birdie's skin is pale, this woman's is tanned and leathery. Birdie is all angles and bold features to the woman's small soft mouth and nose and eyes.

Birdie's first thought is: now they will question me, they will ask me everything, but the woman just smiles at her and says, "It's good to see you feeling better. You'll be up and about soon. You need to get some solid food in you, though." And she gets up and leaves the room and Birdie wonders what she is supposed to do, whether the woman expects her to follow her or what, and she looks down and sees that she's wearing a weird old-lady kind of nightgown with little fabric flowers dotted along the chest. Across the room she sees her own clothes, a black T-shirt and jeans and her boots, draped across a chair. There's nothing else in the bare wooden room but the cot she's lying on, and she gets out of bed and is surprised at how weak she's become. Still, she manages to get over to her clothes, and there's her bag beside it with her phone in it and the few other things she'd brought with her: some graphic novels – *Through the Woods* and *Ms. Marvel* and *Persepolis*, all expertly shoplifted during a school trip to Atlanta because her mother would certainly never buy them for her – her journal, a couple more changes of clothes. She sheds the nightgown and pulls on the clothes she'd been wearing, and right away she feels stronger. The phone is dead. She looks around for an outlet but of course there isn't one. There's probably no electricity at all in this place.

She jumps when the door opens again. It's just the woman coming back, carrying a tray.

"Oh," says the woman. "Look at you up and about! Good for you." She sets the tray down on the bed and Birdie sees there are sliced tomatoes on it and some cold roast chicken and an ear of corn. "The tomatoes and corn we grew," she says proudly. "Not the chicken. Alice got that at the grocery store. But eventually we'll only eat what we grow. We might not have chicken then, though," and Birdie thinks she detects a note of disappointment in the woman's voice. "We're not all vegetarians here, but nobody actually wants to be the one who kills the chicken."

Birdie is surprised at how hungry she is and how much she eats. After she's finished, she takes a deep breath and says, "My name's Birdie." She's never said it out loud before, but just like that, she has her name.

The woman says what hers is as well but Birdie doesn't remember it. She can't. She's so exhilarated to have claimed her name that now she's soaring in the sky, the whole world fallen away below her. She flaps her wings. She flies.

5

She knows she is a bird, at any rate, knew after she heard music by a woman who looked a lot like her and sang a song about her although of course the woman hadn't known about her, not consciously anyway, but somehow she knew enough to make a song about her flying away into the Birdland. Birdie had listened to the song over and over, on the album that had once belonged to her dead sister Donna. She'd downloaded it as well; she often downloaded songs she discovered through Donna's old vinyl collection, but she preferred listening to them in Donna's room, using Donna's things.

Donna had gone missing a good ten years before Birdie was even born, but there were so many pieces of her left behind. Birdie's mother had left Donna's room just as it had been when she vanished: that meant posters of The Cure and The Smiths, *The Hunger* and *The Lost Boys* and *Gothic.* Donna's room had always been off limits to Birdie, but she learned how to use a credit card to jiggle the lock open, and she used to sneak in there when her mother was at work and thumb through Donna's vinyl and play music on Donna's old turntable. Birdie had to be careful to put everything back just as it was because her mother went in there each Saturday and dusted every surface.

Birdie knows Donna is dead. Donna has been dead since long before Birdie was born although for the longest time Birdie had thought she was just gone away, not dead. Birdie had been a late-in-life surprise, as much a shock as Donna had been almost thirty years earlier. Birdie's mother said Donna had been taken from them because she was born in sin, when Birdie's mother was just fifteen years old. Three decades later, Birdie came along, another, different kind of punishment, for what, Birdie's mother wouldn't say, but yet another trial. A test from God.

If that's true, then the same God took away the only person she had ever loved, her grandmother, and Birdie wanted nothing to do with Him.

Birdie isn't yet ready to tell them any of that. Her name, yes, and they took care of her while she was sick so they'll know some of her other secrets too. But her namesake is a secret-secret, and so is Birdland, and everything about Donna and her mother and her grandmother and all the rest.

6

She wakes up again in darkness, though the moon is shining brightly through the open window behind her. It's still hot in there because summer in Georgia is always hot, but it's not the same as the sickly fever heat that had her in its grip for what they tell her was ten days.

Ten days! She wonders what was wrong with her. She's never been sick that long before.

She remembers them reading to her while she was sick – but not her graphic novels or normal books or anything she recognised. Some of the things they read were so odd that surely her fever-brain must have altered them. Words, phrases, ideas linger in her mind like strange shadows at dusk, familiar shapes subtly altered and fading into landscape. As she tries to grasp them they shift and are gone.

There had been people in the room with her at times – a number of them, murmuring or chanting. That must have been part of the fever dreams too. She closes her eyes for a moment and thinks of ancient swollen dying suns, and the sudden quiet that must descend upon a world on the final day of its existence.

The night air coming through the window feels cool for a change, and outside she can hear the calls of the whippoorwills and the tree frogs. There is something inherently melancholic in the noises that the night creatures make, a longing that seems to consume them, maybe because they are consigned to the night or maybe because they mourn the inevitable return of the dawn. Birdie thinks she might be some kind of night bird as well, though definitely not an owl. Owls are wise and friendly and comfortable and she is none of those things.

She can see a brittle half-moon through the window, white and delicate, its cratered surface like lace. Birdie pushes back the thin sheet that's too hot anyway and sits up again. She notices then she doesn't smell, much, after ten days of sweating and sickness, and she thinks they must have bathed her at some point. She remembers stumbling up a couple of times to use the bathroom on her own, only there wasn't a bathroom at all, just an outhouse in the yard beyond the room. She was shocked, but this fits with what she'd heard: *They's a bunch of witches took up living out there in them woods outside of Crosscreek. I heard they was all women. I heard they got that land cheap cause they cast a spell on old Dorsey Ward that sold it to them. I heard they worship the devil. I heard. I heard. I heard.*

Birdie heard, too. She watched and listened and put things away she knew she'd use later, and that talk had been one of those things.

She remembers now from her handful of feverish excursions to the outhouse that she's in an old house, like built in the 1800s old. It's falling apart. Its paint is long gone, and the upper windows that she could see from the back yard are broken or boarded up. The room she's in is as clean as can be, so clearly they are working on making it habitable. Probably they got the land cheap not because they bewitched somebody but because the house was a broken-down ruin without any water or electricity, so anybody normal who bought the place would either have to tear it down and have all the debris hauled off or spend a fortune fixing it up.

Birdie is glad the women bought it. She loves things that are old and forgotten, and suspects they do as well. Living out here, you could forget everything, even time itself. You could raise your own animals and grow your own food and make your own clothes and when you got too old to do any of that, well, then you'd just lay yourself right on down, and sure the world out there would have kept on turning and changing and fighting and hating and dying, but what did that matter, what did any of it ever matter? How was any of it real compared to what was good and solid underfoot, and the soil in your hands and the scent of the night air?

Birdie touches her face, the flesh of her arms. *I'm real. Birdland is real. This place, the Tetractys, they're real.* Everything else, as far as she's concerned, is up for debate.

7

Birdie wanders down the darkened hallway. There are more doors, but people might be sleeping on the other side of them so she leaves them undisturbed. Then the corridor opens up into an entrance hall, and there's a staircase and a front door. She wants to go up the staircase but she hasn't heard anyone moving around up there and maybe they don't use it at all, maybe the staircase and upper floor are rotted. So she opens the door and it's a clear bright night. She can see better than she could inside but not so well that she immediately notices the other person on the porch who says, "Hey."

Birdie about jumps out of her skin. Then she turns and

there's a skinny red-haired girl, not much older than she is, leaning up against the side of the house.

"You're the new girl," she says, or whispers rather.

"I guess," Birdie whispers back.

"I'm Imogen," the girl says, and Birdie just nods and doesn't say her own name because she doesn't know anything about this girl and it might be a trick. You couldn't be too careful.

Faggot. Freak. You're gonna go to hell.

"You make us ten," the girl says.

"What?"

"Didn't you know? The Tetractys – that's all of us, me and Marisa and Winnie and Robin and all the rest – except we weren't, not until you showed up the other day and made ten of us out of nine. Nine's sacred, but it's not like ten, you know? Ten is everything. The goddess, the universe sent you to us."

Birdie thinks about what had made her run: isn't sure she wants to be mixed up with a goddess or universe that set things in motion like that. Didn't sound much better than the god she'd fled with all his tests.

As if she'd read Birdie's mind, Imogen adds, "Figuratively speaking. There's not really a goddess or gods. All of the divine intelligence is in numbers, but you can break all numbers down to 1 and 0. Binary. And right there you have the secret of the universe, encoded. That's why 10 is sacred above all, when you put them together. It's why the Arecibo project used it for transmission. If Creation has a language, it's those two numbers."

Birdie has no idea what the Are-whatsis is, but as the girl talks, the kinds of things that were read to her during her fever-delirium start to come back to her. They sounded like the same kinds of things the girl is telling her. Birdie says, "Where did y'all come from?" She can tell from the girl's way of speaking that she definitely isn't local.

The girl smiles. "We all came from the stars, every one of us. You too." She stuck her arm out. "Look. We're all made from ancient galaxies and other worlds. Someday this world will be gone, and there will be new creatures made out of us, too."

"I meant," Birdie said, "after that."

"We followed the ley lines. They brought us here. But before that, Oregon. And New Jersey, Tennessee, Florida – we're all from different places."

"All right," Birdie said, "so you're here, and now I'm here, so what are you planning to do?"

"Now that we have ten, we are a real tetractys." Imogen sits down next to Birdie and pats the porch for her to do the same. She uses her finger like a pencil to make an imaginary drawing, sketching out a triangle. "A triangle, four rows, ten points, one on top, four on the bottom, two and three in between. Unity, the cosmos. It's all right there in Pythagoreanism."

"That's what they told me," Birdie says, remembered. "When I was sick. They read to me from a book."

Imogen nods. "From Adelaide's journals."

Birdie says, "I don't know what they were."

"She brought us together," Imogen says, "but then she died."

"They read them to me, and I don't remember what was in them."

"Oh, I know what's in them," Imogen says confidently. "Our plans for remaking the world."

8

Birdie wasn't sure how old she was when she first realised there was something wrong with her mother. You didn't notice things like that when you were a little kid because you didn't know anything could be different, and she never had much to compare it to either. She wasn't good at making friends, and she lost the few she had when she did things like go to school with painted nails or wearing makeup (offences that got her sent home as well), so she didn't have a sense of how other families and other mothers acted. All the same, she was sure that even before her grandmother died, she knew there was something *not right* about her mother even if she could not identify what that something was. It wasn't just the way her mother was about her sister's room or the way she seemed to blame Birdie for her life taking the turns it had – even though Birdie had not even existed until her mother was in her forties and could hardly be responsible for the decades of mistakes that had preceded her birth. It was more that there was a peculiar absence about her mother, as though where other people had feelings her mother had the imitation of feelings, toward others at any rate. Birdie suspected her mother felt profoundly sorry for *herself*.

Donna had been eighteen when she vanished. As much as Birdie's mother talked about Donna, she never talked about the circumstances around her disappearance. So Birdie didn't know if Donna had been snatched from her bedroom here or had vanished from the university campus where she went to college or what. She tried looking it up on the internet a few times but found nothing. The local library had old newspapers on microfilm but Birdie only knew that Donna had vanished in 1990, and after spending one disappointing afternoon scanning several months' worth of papers had to admit defeat. She imagined Donna climbing out of her window one night, tying together bedsheets to lower herself to the ground and walking away from their house with all of her belongings knotted up in cloth and tied to a stick like an old-fashioned hobo.

Birdie regretted that she had never really tried to talk to her grandmother about Donna, but she had been just eight years old when her grandmother died. Her grandmother knew a lot more than she let on to Birdie's mother; sometimes Birdie and her grandmother would be alone in a room and Birdie's mother would walk in and Birdie would see that veil fall over her grandmother's eyes and her face go slack like her soul had just gone on a stroll elsewhere. She hadn't looked very different on the cold February morning that Birdie found her dead after bursting into her room like she did on so very many mornings calling out "Granny, Granny, Granny!" That morning, Birdie had stopped. Her grandmother's eyes were open but Birdie knew right away that she was dead. Birdie had felt very little at the discovery; her own experience was that her grandmother had been practising at this for a couple of years, at least, and her soul had finally decided this time that it wouldn't bother returning.

Afterwards a lot of people hugged her and told her how brave she had been and asked her if she was all right, and Birdie struggled away from them as quickly as she could. Even then, before she knew about Birdland, she knew her grandmother had gone someplace far away and better than here.

At least she had a sense of where her grandmother had gone: not like Donna and then her father, both of whom had simply vanished. Birdie used to wonder if they ever thought about her – not that Donna knew she existed, of course, but her father did. In fact, Birdie's mother often darkly implied that Birdie's birth had driven him away from them, but Birdie didn't care and never believed her. She liked to think that Donna and their father might meet out there on the road someday, maybe in some diner, or on the kind of train that you rode for days with compartments you could sleep and eat meals in, or at a lonely crossroads. They'd reunite and make the kind of family that Birdie and her mother never would. And then, when Birdie was old enough, she could set out to find them as well.

Birdie cannot say how it happened that she came to know the truth. It came to her over time, years, a misplaced word here, a contradiction there, and a close, steady observation of her mother. There was no shocking moment of revelation: it began as the seed of an unlikely idea and grew almost without her realising it until one day she looked at her mother, standing across the room with that odd half-smile on her face she sometimes wore, and in that moment she *knew* what her own existence had been punishment for, in her mother's eyes.

She wondered then how her mother had done it. If her father had known, or found out. If her father even was her father, if anything her mother had ever said was true.

How her mother could have done such a thing.

How long it would be until her mother did it to her.

No one would believe her. That much Birdie was sure of. She had read news stories about kids in her situation, kids who said their parents had hurt them and done awful things to them, and nobody ever believed them either.

Birdie touches her neck, almost involuntarily, but the worst of the bruises must have healed while she was sick; the pain is gone. She thinks, *They must be looking for me.* She remembers how much her own hands hurts afterwards, what an appalling amount of strength it had taken, and how much blood there had been. She wants to fly again, but she can no longer remember how to do so. Panic surges through her body. What will become of her if she cannot soar and escape into the sky?

To Imogen, she says, "What would it look like? The remade world, I mean?"

Imogen shrugs "Nobody knows. But it must be better that way, right? The world hurts so much right now. Can you feel it? Maybe it's always hurt that way. I don't know. I haven't been alive that long, but as long as I have been, I've felt it."

Birdie nods.

Imogen says, "You know that feeling you get sometimes? Like you're longing for a person or place that has never existed? Like you just know there's something better, there was supposed to be something better, this wasn't supposed to be the world? A world where, at best, if you are among the luckiest people alive, it only *end*s in pain and sorrow instead of having them as steady companions throughout your life?"

Birdie says, "Like the feeling you get when you look into the sky."

Imogen nods fiercely. She comes over and sits down next to Birdie and pats the porch beside her for Birdie to join her. "Yes," she says. "Yes. The night sky especially. All those stars and all those planets and galaxies and universes and time stretching out and collapsing and making new worlds and you wonder how'd we get so stuck right here? How did we get so sad and angry and lost?"

Birdie sits next to her. "If I was a bird," she says, "I'd be a special kind. One that could leave the atmosphere and fly above the planet. I'd orbit the earth. No, I'd go further. I'd fly into black holes and come out the other side and tell you what I found there."

Imogen says, "You'd be a magnificent bird. I can see you right now, flying through the sky with your hair out behind you like the flag of a pirate ship."

Birdie says, "It's my name, Birdie. I really am a bird."

Imogen takes her hand and says, "I know." Only it isn't a hand any longer, it's the wing of another nightjar, and they are both transformed there together and she lifts Imogen into the sky with her. They skim through the clouds and the lower levels of atmosphere and make for the moon.

9

The tetractys of the decad encompasses the three dimensions, the elements of water, fire, earth, and air, and the music that universes make as they are born, exist, die, and are reborn. At the core of it all is the tenth number, the sacred decad, the union of the 1 and the 0, building blocks of all that will ever be, the transmutation of spirit into matter, here and now and forever.

10

The world ends, the world begins. Not with a whimper, not with a bang.

Birdie opens her eyes. It's dawn. Imogen is still beside her, and their hands are hands again but still gripping one another there on the broken-down front porch of the rotting house. Inside, behind them, the other eight women, the other eight points on the tetractys, are still sleeping.

A flock of birds bursts from treetops, forms an arrow in the sky, climbs toward the heavens. At the last moment, just as they vanish from sight, she sees their formation for what it is: another tetracyts.

The world ends. The world begins. With something as simple as the exhalation of breath. There might be nothing beyond the forest where they sit right now. The end might be rushing near them yet again, and she pictures it flattening trees and turning everything into smoke and nothingness.

Birdie thinks, I am the Queen of Destruction.

She wonders which is about to happen, or has already happened, or will happen soon.

She can't wait to find out.

Twisted Limerick 3

Ramsey Campbell

You'll find that it's worse than a mugger,
That egg that contains a face-hugger.
You may think that you're fine
Till you sit down to dine
And the gripe in your guts is a bugger.

The Fruit of the Tree

Maura McHugh

After Rosa gave birth to her tenth son, Father Augustus visited.

The priest stabbed the rocky path with his cane as he crested the final hill to Rosa's home. The bottom of his cassock, thick with dust, slapped against his boots and added to the cloud that hung about him like a pestilence. The mountain coated his skin, eyelids, and tongue, tasting ancient and acidic.

Augustus had not visited Rosa's aerie before as he'd been warned off by the villagers due to the tasking ascent. Despite his greying hair and stiffening joints he considered himself a fit man, both physically and morally, but as he sweated and gasped up the winding road past the thorn-studded bushes and razor outcrops it was a struggle to banish inappropriate words from his thoughts. Pride, he ruminated, made him avoid this testing ground, when he should have embraced the opportunity to wrestle with his personal demons in order to serve the most wayward of his flock.

He paused at the summit to observe the house: a haphazard building constructed from stone blocks and a thatched roof. It seemed to emerge from the mountain itself. Windows, in differing sizes, gaped in unusual proportions. A grove of the famed gnarled mountain trees grew near a well. Their branches dipped heavy with copper-coloured nuts, considered a delicacy due to their scarcity at lower levels. Pens for pigs and goats huddled about the house, but the goats roamed free, disinclined to be fenced in.

They were the big, local variety with slitted pupils in honey-coloured eyes, thick shaggy pelts in hues of black and russet, and lethal horns that speared back and to the side. They were notoriously wild and difficult to manage, but they appeared content in this lofty abode close to the low clouds. The goats provided the bulk of Rosa's livelihood: the milk and cheese she traded in the village were famous for their rich flavour. Some claimed it had curative properties.

The locals called the breed the dark dancers, due to their agility. Sometimes, Rosa's children were referred to by the same title.

Augustus coughed as he beat his coat to knock the worst of the dust out of it. All the goats turned to stare at him. A big dishevelled beast with a long grizzled beard, perched upon a pillar of stone, stretched his neck down to watch the priest as he strode underneath. Augustus almost reached up for his wide-brimmed hat to secure it, in case the creature decided it wanted a novel meal. But the animal observed his passage without interference.

He knocked on the heavy wooden door with the head of his stick, and the sound echoed around the mountain. Rosa's eldest, Sonatine, opened the door. They had never met, but he'd been pointed out to Augustus when the boy had come to the village with a donkey to collect supplies. Although he was only thirteen he was already as tall as Augustus, and his direct gaze held no deference or welcome. His black hair stood in wild tufts around his bronzed face, making his green, unwavering eyes even brighter.

"Father," he said, with a nod of acknowledgement, and stepped to one side.

Inside the spacious main room seven of the other boys loitered, read, or played with each other. A large, solid table with benches and stools dominated the room. A rough earthenware jug on the mantle above the fire held a mass of frothing meadowsweet flowers, adding a soothing fragrance. Bunches of dried plants hung from the ceiling, and coloured glass jars of roots and herbs were stacked on a dresser. The boys quietened, and stared at him. Augustus stood at the threshold feeling like an intruder, and oddly incapable of entering. There was no sign of the gushing enthusiasm he experienced at most of his parishioners' homes.

"Who's calling?" Rosa's voice drifted from a back room.

"The village confessor," Sonatine replied.

Augustus narrowed his eyes at the boy, but Sonatine's nonchalance deflected his glare.

"Send him in," Rosa said, and added, "and offer him a drink Sonnie. I taught you better."

"Water?" Sonatine asked, "or something stronger?"

"Water, thank you."

Sonatine's lips twitched into a smirk, as if he was amused by the choice. He jerked his head at one of his brothers. They were all remarkably similar in feature and attitude, although their eyes were of different hues. "Breno, show him to Mam." He moved to a large painted pitcher sitting on a trunk. "I'll bring in your *water*."

Breno, lounging on the wide stone window ledge, dropped his book with a sulk, and with barely a glance at the priest sauntered down a long dark hallway, and off that into a big room at the back of the house.

The chamber was cool and dim due to the shutters in the lone window being closed. A thin wedge of dusty sunlight offered the sole illumination. Rosa lay propped up on embroidered cushions on a massive bed with carved posts. Her new baby suckled while a toddler sat at the bottom of the bed chewing on ten thick wooden beads knotted on a rope.

Augustus saw the ripe mound her breast, and averted his eyes.

Rosa smiled, and did not adjust her clothing.

"Good afternoon, Father Augustus," she said. "How brave of you to face the heat and the mountain to meet my wee fellow."

"When on the Lord's business all effort is rewarded."

"And what gift will be granted for this labour?"

For a moment he was flummoxed. He had not expected an interrogation of a stock answer. Rosa observed him with an expression of lively curiosity.

"The sight of another child of the Lord."

She laughed, a merry sound which Augustus thought held a

mocking tone. "A sweet baby's face is certainly pretty to behold. When not screaming."

Rosa inclined her head at a stool by the bed. "Sit, Father, and rest."

Augustus sank down gratefully. Sonatine appeared in the shadowed doorway. He held out a wooden goblet filled with water.

The priest took it, and whispered "*Deo gratias*," before he sipped.

The lad leaned against the doorjamb and watched Augustus drink. "No doubt Mam is the talk of the village," he said.

"There's little to discuss here, except each other," Rosa noted, wryly.

Augustus nodded in agreement. "Ten healthy children is a blessing. Ten boys is a wonder. The midwife tells me you had another easy delivery."

She snorted. "*Easy?* I should wail and thrash more! There's naught easy about giving birth. Babies like blood and pain. The little savages."

The toddler at the end of the bed took the beads out of his mouth, and waved them vigorously for a moment. They clacked loudly.

Rosa grinned at the little boy. "André remembers."

Augustus paused, unsure how to respond to the unorthodox suggestion. He fell back upon scripture to solve the dilemma. "Unto the woman he said, I will greatly multiply thy sorrow and thy conception; in sorrow thou shalt bring forth children."

Rosa's mouth flattened into a line, but she offered no comment.

Augustus used the moment to launch his query. "Will their father be present for the baptism this time, Rosa?"

She shook her head. "He's away."

"He's often away," the priest said. "I checked the records. He hasn't attended any of the Christenings."

"Father Dominick didn't complain."

Augustus resisted the urge to utter an annoyed *tsk*. His predecessor had been notoriously lax in his duties. Before he abandoned them completely. "And there's the matter of your marriage..."

Sonatine walked into the room, and lifted the toddler into his arms. "Come on André, time to milk the dancers."

The child pulled the slimy beads out of his mouth. "Baaa!" he bleated, in a perfect imitation of a goat, and beamed at his brother.

Sonatine smiled, and it was like a sun appearing from behind dark clouds, transforming him into a radiant creature. "Baaa!" he mimicked his brother, and whisked him out of the room.

For a moment the only sound was the babe sucking on his mother's teat. Augustus squirmed.

"There is no marriage certificate," Augustus said, too loudly, and lowered his voice after a glance at the door. "And no note by Father Dominick to explain the matter."

Rosa locked her gaze to his. Her solemn countenance displayed no hint of shame or deceit. "We were joined elsewhere. Father Dominick knew the particulars."

"Did he meet your husband?"

She nodded slowly. "Once."

Augustus frowned. "*Once!* You've had ten children!"

"I know the number of my boys. A perfect decade to manifest mystery."

Her fanciful description only spurred on the priest's anger. Augustus leaned forward, his right hand gripping the head of his cane tight. "You'd be wise to drop such heretical terms, Rosa. None in the village know your husband. Few would even answer questions about him, or you for that matter. Matron Squally had some theories –"

"Aye, I can guess..."

"– but I could not entertain them."

Rosa lowered her head to fix her attention on her baby, and the silence stretched long and uncomfortable between them.

He searched for a safer topic. "Have you decided on a name?"

She brushed a curl of black hair from the baby's forehead. "Cosmas."

"A fine choice."

"His father's."

"He must have been here recently to settle on a name for the babe."

She shook her head. "He sent a message."

Augustus did not try to keep the incredulity from his voice. "You gave birth two days ago. The nearest town is three days' travel!"

Her response was firm, calm. "He sent a message."

Outrage at her dissembling shot him to his feet. He loomed over her. "Give up this coy pretence! Name the scoundrel who fathered this child. And whoever beget the other... illegitimates upon you. Then, the appropriate penance can be set, and your sins absolved."

She did not cower or beg mercy as he expected. Instead she rose to her knees, and levered to her feet to stand on the bed. She stood in the shaft of light, imperious, her form casting a great shadow. Her shift hung loosely, exposing one tanned shoulder. She towered over him.

"Courtesy prevents me from striking you for your manner." Her voice trembled from her anger. "I never cared for the slack-jawed men of the village. Despite how often they have tried to corner me. Rejection poisons their tongues I see."

Augustus stepped back and raised his cane. "You defiant trollop! I will not hesitate to remove your children from this debauched house if you do not either produce your husband," he could not help inserting a laugh, "or name the fathers."

Rosa's face contorted into a visage of fury. She roared, "*SONNIE!*"

The boy appeared instantly, and Augustus guessed he had been listening the entire time.

"Mother," he said, with a downcast gaze.

"The priest wants to meet your sire."

The boy looked up quickly, his eyes wide with surprise. "But —"

She bellowed at him, "*Arrange it!*"

It was too much for the baby: it detached from her nipple and began to scream. Rosa inhaled a deep breath, and stroked the cheek of her son in the crook of her arm, before she glared at the priest. "Get out," she ordered, her voice hoarse.

Sonatine backed into the hallway, and Augustus followed him. He was shaking from anger, but curiosity was overtaking his shock at Rosa's behaviour. Never had he been treated so by a common wench. He had not expected her to hold onto her lie so fiercely.

Augustus imagined Sonatine would escort him out of the house and down to the door of his father in the village, but instead the young man dithered in the hallway. Finally, he muttered "Wait here," and dodged up the hallway to the kitchen.

Augustus glanced back at the doorway to Rosa's bedroom. He could hear her shushing Cosmas, who was already calming down. She began singing a song with a peculiar melody in a strange tongue. An involuntary shiver rolled through his body. An instinct to bolt from the house seized him, but he overpowered it with his righteous certainty. Rosa would be exposed as a viper nesting high above his respectable, unsuspecting parishioners. If she remained unchecked, she would strike at their decent hearts eventually. The boys could still be saved – the younger ones at least.

Sonatine appeared, holding a silver and glass lamp in which a green candle burned.

"What's this?" Augustus asked, "I don't need a light. The kitchen is a few steps ahead."

"We're not going that way," the boy replied, his voice low and irritated. He raised the lamp, and pushed past the priest and down the hallway, past three open doors. They led to the boys' bedrooms, each containing several beds, and a scattering of toys and clothing.

The hallway turned left, and right, before it veered sharply left again. The darkness was absolute. The temperature plunged. Before them another passageway stretched with no end in sight from the comfort of the circle of lamplight. Augustus laid his hand upon a wall. It was smooth stone, piercingly cold. He yanked his hand away, his palm burning.

He stopped. "Where are we going?" he demanded, using the authoritative voice that made his followers jump to his bidding.

Sonatine turned. He held the lamp high, and it washed out his features. "You asked to see him. I will take you."

"We're going into the mountain."

The boy nodded. Then he turned and walked briskly forward, carrying the light with him.

Augustus hurried, not wishing to be left behind in the shadows.

The further they walked down the long corridor the more Augustus became convinced he could hear a whispering sound. It was like an animated conversation between people taking place out of sight, their indistinct words betraying their sly presence. He dropped his hand on the boy's shoulder and stopped him.

"Can you hear it?" he asked.

They waited, their breathing quiet, but silence and darkness bound them in. Shortly, the stillness produced a weight that suffocated. Augustus imagined the mass of the mountain above and around them, pressing down upon the narrow space. Panic beat in his chest, which now seemed too tight to suck in air.

"We must leave," he managed to squeeze out, trying to keep his terror out of his voice.

"She told me to take you to him," Sonatine said.

"What is his name?"

"He has many," Sonatine replied, "and you have heard them all before." With that he moved on quickly. Augustus had to hurry to catch up with the bubble of light.

After a long march they arrived at a solid wall on which was carved an arched doorway. At its centre a series of concentric circles were drawn – like ripples spreading outward from a stone dropped in a black pool.

"What's this?" asked Augustus. He could hear the quaver in his voice, but his fear was a great master, whipping him on with a stick, and he could do nothing to escape its floggings except race along with it.

"The gate."

Augustus backed up, he was certain now that to go any further would be to damn his soul. He prepared to flee back down the pitch-black hallway. Even if he must navigate the darkness by touch alone it would lead him to the surface, eventually.

Sonatine turned to face him, and in his eyes the light of the lamp gleamed like salvation.

"You cannot leave yet, Augustus," the boy said, but his voice was that of his mother. "You are expected. If you run you will be trapped in a maze of perpetual night. You will die slowly, alone in the dark, confined by the mountain."

Sonatine smiled his mother's smile. "I am the way, and if you follow me, you will know the truth."

The boy turned and laid his left hand upon the circle in the centre of the gate. The groove around it lit up with a green glow. Each of the larger circles shone in turn, until they met the outline of the archway.

All the rings suddenly flashed a brilliant light, blinding Augustus with bright circles etched into his vision.

When his sight cleared he stood before an open stone gateway, and beyond it a tunnel, laced with luminescent fronds, which moved gracefully as if stirred by a breeze, and shifted through the colours of the rainbow in gradual waves.

Sonatine had vanished. Gone ahead, Augustus hoped. He turned his head to glance at the hallway behind him. There was nothing to see except a barrier of black.

He stepped into the tunnel, and it felt as if a latticework of spongy roots lay underfoot. The floor dipped down gradually as he walked forward. He could not identify the plants growing on all sides. They were varieties of moss or mushroom, and some of them had pearl-like glistening drops at their tips. A sweet fragrance permeated the space, lulling him. Soon Augustus felt more relaxed, and his breathing became freer. He drifted along the tunnel following a pull that grew within him until it became a vital urge.

Ahead of him the tunnel opened out into a massive radiant chamber covered in the glowing plants. Its steady mesmeric pulse of changing hues felt like a heartbeat. At the centre stood a gigantic tree trunk, with vine ropes knotted around it. Augustus craned his neck back but he could not discern its top. Further up, immense boughs arched out to connect to the chamber's walls. There was only awe at the majesty of the shining place.

Sonatine stood in the fork of an enormous root. His unruly hair had unfurled out and waved around his face. He was tiny against the vastness of the tree – another pod in a sea of polyps.

Augustus approached him, and more questions crowded his mind.

Sonatine laid his hand upon the root, and a lattice of vines erupted to form the framework of a face. From them leaves and berries burst, creating the flesh of a face, eyes, and mouth.

"This is my father," said Sonatine.

A sound reminiscent of forest leaves rustling in a breeze sprang up, and Augustus guessed it was meant to be an expression of amusement.

The glossy plant lips moved. "And your mother," it said. The leaves subtly shifted and altered until it modelled Rosa's features.

Augustus shook off the wonder that saturated his mind, distracting him from his mission. This ran counter to the teachings he had followed his entire life.

Before Augustus could interject, the mask of leaves continued: "We are the seed of the mountain, and within all mountains reside such seeds. We communicate across the array of life rooted in the earth, just as all people are connected by their chain of progeny."

"You are our child, Augustus. Less directly than our ten, but you are a related scion."

A vine slithered over his boot and wrapped around it. A red thorn pushed out and pierced the leather with ease, and his skin beneath it. After a sharp pain it numbed instantly.

The whispering returned, but it was now a song of voices in his mind: a melody comprised of many phrases and elements, which vibrated in his blood and bones. It was a hymn to all of creation, and it showed him his place within the community of the choir.

"No!" With the strength of his training, Augustus willed the song into a murmur in his mind. He looked down and realised his body was covered in vines. Several grew up to coil lightly around his neck and brush across his cheeks. He wanted to struggle against his cage, but was incapable of movement. A feathery touch on his forehead warned him that the vine was sprouting thread-like roots.

The great tree continued. "From our spores your minds expanded for the first time, pushing beyond the veils of ignorance. You died and we absorbed your experiences, allowing us to know your short, mobile lives. Your deities sacrificed themselves upon our trees to gain our insights, and we granted them so you could return to us and enrich us further. You are our compost and our fruit."

The roots borrowed into the priest's skin, and they reconnected him to that first grand experience: floating within his mother's womb, his body growing from hers, and within her the millions of lives which had germinated before.

He could follow that sequence of lives down to its most minute, floating through space, a dormant speck from another world, shed from the great tree in another of its varied manifestations. There was no end or beginning, but a series of expressions. Even if all life was to terminate on this planet, the waves of particles continued to flow throughout the universe, bringing with it potential for a fresh flowering, and carrying all knowledge of what went before packed into a condensed kernel.

And within Augustus the primordial tree planted a seed.

When it fed upon the fertile soil in which it was embedded, Augustus emerged transformed, damp and shivering, from the withered matrix of vines.

Sonatine waited for him.

The boy knelt, and gently combed his fingers through the short hair covering Augustus' new body.

"Easy," Sonatine whispered, "you will settle in time."

Augustus flicked long ears, and stamped four hooves. Memories from a previous existence slipped away as when one wakes from a dream. Now, new demands and imperatives asserted themselves.

Mostly she was young and thirsty.

And the tree's mask spoke, finally. "You will grow and gain the wisdom of this body, give birth, and return to the earth, so we will know your existence, and prepare for the next one."

Sonatine stood, and the baby goat gazed up at him with the trust of the innocent.

"Come on, Aggie," Sonatine said, slapping his thigh as encouragement.

The kid followed the boy out of the centre of the mountain, eager for nourishment.

Twisted Limerick 4

Ramsey Campbell

You may get yourself into a stew
With the chap who's just one big tattoo.
He is covered with tales,
And you'll find your heart quails
When you see the last one's about you.

9 + 1

Michael Marshall Smith

1. The garden of 427 Cedar Street. I was resident there at
   the time.

2. The northern end of a gulley four hundred yards from the
   northern end of town. Rough sketch attached.

3. The ocean, off Wilder Ranch, about a mile off Highway 1.

4. In a hillside, close to Davenport Landing. Sketch
   attached.

5. An area of redwood forest in the Santa Cruz mountains,
   approximately half a mile from Empire Grade Road, two
   miles from Felton. More detailed sketch attached.

6. See (5)

7. See (5) and (6)

8. The rear garden of my grandmother's house in Half
   Moon Bay.

9. In three canvas bags in marshland close to the East
   Bridge over the San Lorenzo river. Unfortunately I was
   unable to get to the location specified in 5/6/7 on
   account of a party of students drinking nearby. Several of

them were clearly under 21 years of age.

10. I cannot allow myself to do this any more. I do not even know who 9 was. I saw her coming out of CostCo and followed her and it happened the same night, which is too fast. I had observed the other women for some time. If it has come to this — if it can occur without the protocol I had developed in the last three years — then there is no reason for it to ever stop and I understand this is unfair to the community at large. My grandmother raised me very inappropriately and she should have been the end. She was not and it has become what I am and so there can be no conclusion except this one. You will find me at the same location specified for 5, 6, 7. I am sorry for the trouble I have caused. Please act upon this letter swiftly because I have a great fear of my body being consumed by animals, which I accept is ironic given the things you will find in my freezer.

Sincerely,
Matthew Jones.

Twisted Limerick 5

Ramsey Campbell

Better see you don't upset the kid!
He's had fun with the people who did.
With the power he can wield
He dumped one in a field
In a shape that we all wished were hid.

The Book of Sleep

Edward Cox

She tries to save them. She is the Healer, but her world is diseased.

Through fields of failing crops, she leads the people to the edge of chalk cliffs, where there is nowhere left to run, where hopes of reaching safety end. Far below, the sea swells and roars upon sharp rocks; high above, the clouds are black as starless night. The sky is lost, the land is dying, and the people wail and moan in despair. So many of them – young and old and broken.

"It's me you're looking for!" the Healer shouts at the sky. "These people are innocent!"

Her only answer is a bellow of thunder and she knows that it is too late. Iron grey talons of lightning claw over the blackness. More wails. More moans. And then the rain comes. In streaks of green, the sky bleeds emerald fire which cannot be doused. The world is aflame. The Healer weeps as the people burn. Some of them choose the quick end of the wild sea below. Others scream as the salty air ignites. The Healer is helpless to protect them. This is her dream, and the Nightmares have come.

"Why did you stay?" she says. And she is looking directly into my eyes as the sky falls around her. "I told you to leave –"

I awoke in the temple, discovering that I had sleepwalked to the eastern Vigil Hall. The flutter of torch flames barely lifted the shadows. The air was cold and damp. The wind sighed distantly beyond the walls. In my hand, the wand glowed with the light of paradise, vibrating with power, silver-blue and warm to the touch. The only conscious soul in the temple, I stood strong and ready, as I did every night, devoutly the defender.

The warning I received in my dream visions was always the first sign. The second came when the torches began to burn low, their flames turning from yellow to green. The third took the form of unintelligible voices, whispering with the bitterness of winter, chilling my skin to gooseflesh. The last sign was the sand. It poured in from between great stone blocks, hissing, creating small dunes on the hall's flagstones. And from these dunes, the Nightmares manifested and rose.

On this night the apparitions came as perversions of men, featureless ghouls formed from millions of golden grains. Too many to count, they filled the spacious Vigil Hall, swaying on their feet, glinting in the green light as if studded with tiny jewels. Their cold whispering became the buzz of an angry swarm, and as one they shuffled towards me.

Aiming the wand, I felt no fear, only a calm dedication to duty. The wand's trigger released a bolt of divine magic, merciless, crackling like lightning as it surrounded the nearest Nightmare with its wrath. Sand heated and smoked, and the apparition dissolved to dust. The next fell, and then the next, as I trod backwards carefully, pulling the trigger, leading the horde down the passageway out of the Vigil Hall. Without urgency, the Nightmares followed, almost obliviously lumbering into purifying blazes of magic.

They had no interest in me. I doubted they were even aware of my presence. It was the Healer they wanted. Night after night they came, seeking to invade her sleep, feed upon her dreams, poison her mind. I alone stood in their way, and they had no defence against the divine weapon in my hand.

The passage was narrow, corralling the Nightmares into a densely-packed line of shambling figures, a small army of sand men. Their angry voices deafened me; the fury of the wand blinded me; scorched sand choked me.

One after the other, the Nightmares dissipated. I kept firing, kept moving backwards, until I took my first steps into the Inner Sanctum, the heart of the temple where the Healer slept in her chariot. Eyes watering, retreating no more, I ensured that no Nightmare made it out of the passage. The aroma of divine magic was clean yet angry, full of rage and justice. By the time the last apparition fell to grains of smouldering sand, the light of the wand had waned to a dull twilight glow, and the silence was total.

Still as a statue, I waited as energy rushed by me. Not a wind as such, but a magical void that sucked burnt and smoking sand away down the passage, drew it back into gaps between stone blocks. The torches fluttered and their tall yellow flames returned.

Giving thanks to God for providing the strength and power to battle the Nightmares once again, I turned, wearily, and approached the Healer's chariot.

It sat at the centre of the Inner Sanctum. Ovoid, shining and metallic, looking almost like a giant egg laid by some mythical beast, resting on four thick silver legs. Its aura tingled on my skin as I pressed the sacred seal. The door appeared and lowered to form steps up into the Healer's private chamber. Heavenly secrets greeted me with the intricacies of a higher science I could scarcely comprehend.

My first duty, as always, was to return the wand to its proper place. The weapon clicked into its housing. Multi-coloured lights danced and blurred in rainbow hues through the silver panel surrounding it. The glow of the wand flared and dimmed as it replenished spent magic. Next, I bowed my respect to the Healer herself.

She slept at the back of the chamber, in a tank shaped like a sarcophagus, surrounded by more rainbows. Through frosted glass I could see her silhouette drifting in luminous fluid, submerged in the memory of heaven and God's love. Haunted and alone, she had only me to protect her from her own dreams. Sometimes I wept for her loneliness, but I never stopped feeling proud to serve her. To fight for her.

Wishing the Healer peace in her sleep, I left the chariot and made the short walk to the northern sanctum, *my* sanctum.

Drawing water from the well there, I washed sand from my

skin, and drank away the stigma of the night. Sitting at my table, I wrote my thoughts and experiences down onto the pages that would further the narrative in the Book of Sleep. It was then that a coughing fit shook me. Blood spattered the parchment. I wiped it from the page and my lips with a trembling hand. Red glistened in the torchlight.

Before retiring to my cot and resuming my sleep, praying for visions that were not sullied by the Healer's Nightmares, I made my final entry.

The time has come, I wrote. *I am dying.*

It is written that she came to do God's work. It is written that God sent her to spread wisdom and heal the sick. Which she did. For a time.

The Healer is tending to the people of the First Settlement, those who witnessed her descent from the sky. It is a simple community at a time when scattered farmsteads line the coast, before a city of stone rose up and swallowed them all. It is winter. A clean sun blazes above snow dusted fields. Dark clouds loom on the horizon, drifting landward over the bitter sea with the inexorable promise of fresh flurries. Wrapped up against the cold, the people have flocked to the Healer. A sickness has broken out among them, its symptoms present in old and young alike. They are afraid.

They congregate close to the cliffs, where the Healer's chariot stands. Oval and shining, as grey as the distant clouds, the chariot braves the elements along with the people, for this is a time before the temple had been built. Fires burn and smoke. Groups huddle around warming flames, backs turned to the stiff sea wind. Children cry. Adults comfort them.

The Healer moves among the people administering medicine; little white stones that could have been chipped from the cliff's chalk face. She is aided by her druids – those to who she has taught the art of healing. The Healer dresses like the people, speaks like them. Her face looks both like and unlike theirs, beautiful yet somehow not of this world. She is heavenly, God's angel, and her smiles are full of hope as she sends families back to their farms and homesteads with promises that the sickness will soon pass.

Slowly the crowd thins until the druids escort the last of the people back to their homes. Looking at the ominous clouds drifting over cold swells, the Healer offers her smile to me. "This was a happier time," she says. Her eyes seem to see inside my soul, and her smile is sadder than before. "You are ill. You are suffering."

"I suffer willingly." It was rare for the Healer and me to converse without the looming threat of her Nightmares. When we did, I experienced the most joyous moments of my vigil. "But I feel no pain. Not here. Not with you."

"Even if I were awake, I could not heal you, defender. Your sickness is beyond God's medicine."

"All mortals die. My only wish is to live long enough to see you awakened and returned to the people."

The Healer tilts her head to one side. "And if you do not?"

"Then I will die your defender, and my soul will sing your name in heaven."

My words are proud, but there is pity on the Healer's face, a tear in her eye.

"The people who first welcomed me died generations ago," she says. "Why have the rest of you remained? I did not want this."

"We stayed to protect you." This is not the first time the Healer has asked that question, and it breaks my heart whenever I am compelled to answer. How can she not understand our devotion? Why does she feel unworthy of our love? "We remain loyal to repay all that you gave us."

"All I have given *you* is a sickness that cannot be cured." Gulls cry, flying from the approaching storm. The Healer frowns at the horizon, seems suspicious of the snow clouds. "One day, God's angels will come for me. And when that day arrives —"

The clean sun suddenly burns brighter, fiercer, and I shield my eyes from its glare.

"Morning has come," the Healer says. Through the blinding light, I can barely see her walking to the chariot. "Time to wake up, defender."

A deep rumble dragged me from sleep. The temple doors had opened.

By the time I heard them close again, I had washed and dressed and travelled from the northern end of the temple to the southern hall, where I stood before the Dreamer Gate – the penultimate barrier between me and the outside world. It was morning, but there were no windows through which sunlight might shine. In this temple, I could only acknowledge the passage of time through daily rituals and the chronicles I wrote. Ten years had passed since I last saw the sky, the moon and stars, the sea, the city... my people. But I would see them all again soon. Just once more.

The Dreamer Gate was a great slab of dark and smooth stone. Upon it was written the story of the Healer. As I had so many times before, I waited for the gate to open while studying the words and pictures engraved upon it by the chisels of my ancestors.

It was written that the people had been afraid before she came. A mighty storm had raged for ten days, and they had believed that some blaspheme had been committed to incur God's wrath. But then he had sent the Healer to them. It was written that she rode her chariot through clouds of blackest night, fierce lightning and raindrops the size of giants' tears. It was written that when she came the storm had stopped. She had embraced the people with love and wisdom, and the very earth was blessed by her presence.

Another rumble. Dust swirled around me. My ears were filled with grind of stone on stone. The Dreamer Gate slid to one side, revealing the opening to the storage chamber. Inside, I found the morning's delivery.

This small room was opened to me for one hour a day. On the other side, the stone doors to the outside world were closed and sealed. I never saw who came here every day, never got the chance to say, "Thank you," for the sack of fresh food they left; for the sheets of parchment, the pot of ink, the barrel of spare torches. I took the new delivery back to my chamber, and in return I left the pages that I wrote the previous night for the Book of Sleep. The pages that informed the druids that my time in the temple was coming to an end.

In my chamber, I lit the stove and boiled a pan of water. From the sack I took some dried herbs and petals, which I added to the pan to brew a medicinal beverage to sooth a throat that all too often these days felt raw and rough as bark. There were also strips of dried meat in the sack – too tough for my loose teeth to chew, so I tenderised them in another pan of boiling water. I found a loaf. The crust was hard and blackened, but the bread inside was soft, freshly baked and still warm. Thankful for what I had been given, I ate my breakfast, though it had become difficult for me to stomach any food at all.

There wasn't much for me to do in the temple during the day. I had my regular chores and routines, but mostly I was alone with my thoughts. Isolation so often played tricks on the mind, but whenever I questioned my sanity, whenever loneliness brought me to my lowest ebb, I meditated upon the reason I was here. The reason why I was separated from my people, why I had turned my back on a life without confinement or finding a partner or raising children...

The Healer.

For decades she had cared for the people. She made the blind see and cripples walk. She gave sanity to the mad and banished disease. Word of her wisdom and healing spread across the land. More and more people came, flocking to the Healer as though she were a beacon of hope, of goodness – which she was. And they were awed and blessed to lay eyes upon this angel of God, who sought no reward her divine work.

A generation of druids learned from her teachings; and in turn, they – proficient now in the art of healing – taught the next generation. The Healer witnessed the First Settlement become a village that became a town. But she never saw the city arise; she never knew that a temple had been built around her chariot. Because as good and healthy as the Healer made life for everyone, she herself grew old and tired.

It was written that the Healer slept the long sleep in her chariot so she could bathe in the magic of heaven and replenish her youth and strength. It was written that her parting message to the people was for them to leave her be, to never disturb her sleep. She promised to return to them, when she was ready. But the Healer had not awoken for more than two hundred years. The people prayed every day for her return, but every day those prayers were only answered by her Nightmares.

After my breakfast, I wandered the temple, tending to my daily duties. I replaced spent torches. The glare of their flames and smoke stung my eyes. Taking a bucket of water and some rags to the Inner Sanctum, I washed and polished the Healer's chariot. By the time I had finished, silver metal glinted with reflected fire.

I had just stepped back to admire the chariot – weary and ailing but pleased with my work – when my nose began to run with blood.

Hurrying to my chamber, I stemmed the flow with rags, and prepared myself for the inevitable coughing fit. When it came it was a furnace raging in my chest. I hacked more blood into my hands, struggling for breath with each bark.

The attack didn't last long. After, I cleaned myself and rested a while on my cot, drifting into twilight but not quite falling asleep. When the pain in my chest subsided to a slow, quiet burn, I rose, wrapped in my blanket. I drank another medicated brew and dipped the last of the bread into a pot of honey that I found at the bottom of the sack.

My sickness – it wouldn't go away. It was beyond the skills of the druids, who served and taught in the city as the Healer's legacy. For they were only mortal. My sickness was the sacrifice that we defenders willingly made. To defend the Healer, to protect her from the Nightmares, we wielded the wand, the magic of heaven, and such power was not meant for the likes of us. Prolonged use took a toll upon our bodies. Over time, it killed us.

Along with the frequent nose bleeds and bloody cough, I had lost my hair and I was losing my teeth. The fevers weren't so frequent, nor were the weeping sores that appeared on my skin, but every day I could feel myself getting weaker and weaker. Soon, the druids would send someone younger and healthier to the temple, a new defender to continue the vigil. Perhaps tonight I would make my final entry in the Book of Sleep. Perhaps tomorrow I would feel the sun, the wind, the rain on my face, and make preparation for my soul's journey to heaven.

I felt strong enough to spend the afternoon sharpening scribers and pouring dregs of ink from the old pot into the new. I washed my clothes and blankets in cool, clean water from the well, and hung them up to dry. All the while, I wondered if this would be my last day as the defender. So many of us, stretching back to the old times and the first of us. We druids had little dealings with politics and royalty and city business. We led a simpler, purer life, dedicated to medicine and the preservation of the Healer's wisdom. For the past ten years all I had known was the flicker of torchlight and the cold grey stone that surrounded me.

The temple had been built before the city had been completed, but not as a monument to the Healer. Its purpose was to contain her Nightmares. When she had first fallen asleep, the people feared that the ghosts and apparitions that sprang nightly from her dreams were demons sent by the Serpent Lord to taunt and prey upon a weakened angel. But one druid knew the truth.

He had lived as a hermit, in a cave near the chariot. He had been the first defender, the Healer's guardian, the only druid permitted to enter the chariot – the most sacred of all places. It was written that the Healer sent him visions to help him understand that her sleep was troubled. The demons were Nightmares, manifested from her dreams; and each time they arose, the first defender fought them with the magic of heaven. And he continued to fight until the sickness took him and a new defender was chosen from among the druids. I was the latest in a proud lineage to take up the vigil.

My chores done, I prepared the last of the dried meat, and ate my final meal of the day. I tried not to think about death as I waited for what the night would bring.

The wand blazed. A gout of sand erupted, sparkling and smouldering before hissing to the flagstones with a sound like rain. Low and deep green flames struggled to rise from torches. My nose bled, my chest burned like a furnace. The wand spat magic again and again, but I was firing blindly, desperately. Sand filled my eyes, my mouth, mixing with the blood that had risen from my throat. I could barely breathe and my strength was already failing.

The Nightmares had risen in the western Vigil Hall as a single beast. A great monster with a fat powerful body; its legs stocky and thick. Its wide head and long face was lined with horns, and its mouth was a gaping abyss. Its voice was a bellow that shook the temple to its foundations.

Its tail lashing wildly, the beast was surrounded by a biting tempest of sand that pushed me further and further into retreat, back along the passageway that led to the Inner Sanctum. Perhaps my sickness had made me weaker than I realised, but the fight had never been this hard to maintain before. The Nightmares were so focussed, so... vicious, and the wand barely held them at bay. Clear shots at the beast were difficult. Each time divine magic achieved a direct strike, my foe shrank but kept its form, and continued shrinking until it was small enough to gallop down the passage and charge me.

We met in a clash of magic and searing sand. Blood frothed from my throat, choking my cry of defiance. Heat and smoke enveloped me. Madly, blindly, I kept pulling the wand's trigger until I fell into a darkness that not even the light of paradise could penetrate.

The pain has gone.

The Healer stands upon the cliffs, looking out to sea. The sun is setting, its fading red light struggling to shine through clouds as thick and black as pitch. Waves crash against the rocks far below. The wind carries the bite of winter and salt. There are tears in the Healer's eyes, but she does not blink, does not stop staring at the dark, blood-smeared horizon.

"Stories and beliefs have a habit of blurring the edges of the truth," she tells me. "It's true that I asked the people not to disturb my sleep, but I never promised to return. I told them to leave, to get as far away from me as possible." She shakes her head. "Why didn't they listen to my warning? How many thousands now live in the city?"

I look away from the sea and into the near distance, down into the valley where the city rises. Darkness has already cast its shroud across the land, and the buildings and towers are silhouettes, pinpricked with twinkling jewels of firelight. Years ago, while preparing for my vigil, I had often sat by the temple to gaze at the city. It looks exactly as it had the last time I did so. This vision must be of the present. Strange; the Healer has only ever shown me the old days before.

"You wished us to leave?" I ask her. "Did we offend you?"

"No." The answer is true, heartfelt.

"Then... I don't understand."

The Healer is quiet for a long moment. The clouds thicken on the horizon. The red of the sun dulls.

"What would you say if I told you that God didn't send me?" she says. "What if I told you that I was lost? That I fell to this place where... heaven could no longer see me?"

What would I say? "You... are God's angel." My frown is troubled. "And God sees all."

She smiles wryly at that, and whispers, "God sees all... eventually."

Closing her eyes, she faces up to the sky and takes a deep breath of sea air. Where the clouds have not yet reached, stars decorate the heavens. The moon's silver light is radiant upon the Healer's skin.

"There was a time when I was one of many angels watching your world," she says, as if confessing to the sky. "We rode a mighty ship that could sail among the stars. We observed, but we were forbidden to interfere with your lives. God's secrets were not for you."

"There were more healers?" I ask uncertainly.

"Healers, philosophers, builders, gardeners, historians – and they all died. Catastrophe struck our ship, you see. It was destroyed, ripped apart, and its debris is now scattered amongst the stars we once sailed. I alone escaped in my chariot."

She stares out at the horizon, her face carved from stone, remorse in her voice. "I hid at first. I upheld our laws, didn't show myself to the people, vowing to reveal not one of our secrets. Distressed and lost, I called to heaven, begging for rescue. But heaven did not hear me. No one replied. No one came. So I made a choice."

She looks down at the sea. "I showed myself to the people. My chariot was not built to travel the stars, and I was certain that I would spend the rest of my life on this world. So I chose to break our laws, to live among you, to teach you heaven's secrets."

I struggle with words, opening my mouth but finding nothing to say. There had been more angels? Angels that could die? The Healer was lost, not sent by God? And heaven would turn its back on one of its own divine creatures? It makes no sense. Nothing of this is written in the Book of Sleep.

"Your sickness is my sickness, defender. My chariot is broken, and I cannot be awakened now." The Healer's eyes bore into my soul, and she sheds a tear for the confusion and fear she sees there. "I didn't sleep because I was old and tired, I did so because I made the wrong choice. Heaven *had* heard my call, but its reply took many years to reach me. And now... God's angels are coming."

"Angels are coming?" I shake my head, wondering if this vision is the work of Nightmares. "Will they take you from us?"

"I made grave mistakes, defender." The Healer's expression is a mixture of pity for me and shame for herself. "I was wrong to reveal heaven's secrets. I was wrong to change so much in your world. I told the people to abandon me because the angels will repair the damage I have done."

"*Damage?*"

She cuts me off. "God cannot allow your world to benefit from the higher science of a greater evolution –"

A shout of thunder interrupts her.

The Healer sighs. "They are here."

The horizon screams, shaking the ground. Black clouds burst, roiling with golden fire. I sink to my knees, cowering before so much power, barely understanding an overwhelming sense of finality that has sunk down into my dying bones. Lightning spits at the sea. Fire and darkness part. Through the void comes a great chariot that races towards the land.

Impossibly huge, a behemoth disc of silver-blue, so large it could block the sky. And I know that it is a divine ship built for sailing among the stars. Its fat edge glows red, its passing angers the sea into frothing waves of rage. The wrath of God comes with it, an all-consuming menace which cannot be denied; and although its voice is a deafening roar that threatens to burst my eardrums, the Healer's voice rises effortlessly above even this.

"Take my hand, defender," she says, and she pulls me to my feet. "An unimaginable distance lies between your world and heaven. For more than two hundred years this ship has been travelling, searching for me." She speaks breathlessly. With fear? "The angels have the power to send many souls to heaven."

The ship comes ever closer, showing no signs of slowing. It rains fire; its roar might shake the land apart.

"They will take my soul?" I whimper.

"Yours and those of every man, woman and child living in the city."

Her words conceive a joyous occasion, but her tone is filled with dire warning. By the hand, she leads me to the very edge of the cliff. The wind is bracing; the grey waves crash against the cliff face, pushed higher before the power of the behemoth ship.

The Healer says, "The angels are my Nightmares, defender. The Book of Sleep ends tonight." She squeezes my hand, and her beautiful eyes brim with tears, her ageless face is beset by sadness. "I am sorry."

Together, we jump into the sea.

I awoke to a deep, consuming pain inside me. Rolling to my side, I vomited bloody sand. Coughing threatened to shatter my body.

At first, I thought I could still hear the terrible roar of heaven's behemoth ship. But I realised that it was the Dreamer Gate that I heard, opening and closing. Was it morning already? No, I could feel that this was still night. Did the temple have intruders?

I was too weak to move. Still lying in the passageway where I had fallen, I looked beyond the darkness into the torchlight flickering in the Inner Sanctum. I heard footsteps scratching over sand. More coughing shook me. I groaned at the agony. And then I saw them.

The Healer had shown me no mere vision or dream; she had shown me the truth. The angels had come.

I saw two of them in the torchlight. One was much taller than the other, both were dressed in suits of silver, their heads and faces concealed within bowls of what seemed to be dark grey metal or glass – it was hard to tell with the light reflecting so brightly from them. As the tall angel strode over to the Healer's chariot, the short one entered the passageway and approached me. In fear and panic and pain, I froze.

In the darkness, the angel's breastplate radiated a soft glow that pulsed with a blur of hues. The figure stopped two paces from me, the dark shell of its head tilting one way and then the other as it considered me, perhaps sensing how close to death I was. A part of me acknowledged how awed I felt to be in the presence of God's servant; but the voice of the Healer raced through my mind, the sadness in her tones, the warning in her words... *The Book of Sleep ends tonight.*

My confusion deepened, despair gripped me.

"Will –" I coughed sand and blood from my throat. "Will you take my soul to heaven?" My voice was a lonely creak.

By way of reply, the angel crouched and picked up the wand, which lay just out of my reach. Its magic had not been replenished after the last battle against the Nightmares. Its divine power was all but spent, its glow barely shining. The angel turned from me and walked to the Inner Sanctum, carrying the wand. I tried to rise but failed pitifully. Dredging up whatever strength remained in me, I resorted to dragging myself after the angel, clawing through the pain.

When I reached the Inner Sanctum, blood was streaming from my nose. I collapsed. The door of the chariot was open and both angels were inside. I could see them, but not what they were doing. They didn't linger, however, and were soon finished. My vision blurred by tears, I watched them leave the chariot and head down the passage that led to the Dreamer Gate, without so much as sparing me a glance.

"Please," I croaked after them, my throat raw and withered. "What of the people?"

Perhaps they answered me, perhaps they did not. I passed out and regained consciousness to hear a strange sound.

As if the Healer herself were singing to me, the chariot emitted a series of soft coos – a single note, repeated over and over, growing in tempo, building to finality. It seemed to cool the molten metal in my chest and bones, steady my breathing, and lull me towards sleep. The Healer sang faster and faster until her coos became a long continuous wail, and the chariot erupted with the fire of God.

I saw it: silver-blue and liquid, pouring onto the flagstones, coming for me. I knew it would break down the temple, rush into the valley, consume the city, and swallow thousands of souls into the glory of heaven. I experienced a blinding flash of divine light, which seemed both momentary and eternal. And before brief pain brought an end to my suffering, I knew that the Nightmares were dead and the Book of Sleep had concluded.

My vigil was over.

Twisted Limerick 6

Ramsey Campbell

Don't forget to bring Algernon flowers!
Let me ask while I still have my powers.
As my speech slips away
I'll have much less to say –
Me and mouse, them big wurds arnt ours.

For The Win

James Barclay

"Bullshit. He was mine."

"In your dreams. You just can't handle that fact you're losing."

"I'm just disappointed that a sibling of mine would stoop to such an obvious lie." My mind is cramped from arcing, aching from our time in the Flux. "Also, I'm not losing. I never lose."

"Sour grape stench everywhere, Big-Sis."

"Don't call me that, Little Prince." I hate the way he does that. Always saying it like it's my fault, my choice to be bigger and his sister. "One of these days..."

"Can't hurt me, I'm family," he says. "Besides, we're a Two."

And so we are but it's not as if I really had a choice and if I had my time again I'd have held out for a total stranger. Alyn is a wheedling moron sometimes but he's a really talented wheedling moron, and when he showed the vision so young and took to the training so effortlessly... and because he's my brother then what other decision could I have made? What other decision would Father have let me make?

Everyone had smiled and said what a Two we'd make and they were right of course, because we're awesome. But they all forgot that it means I have to live with my wheedling moron little brother every minute of every long, whining day. Don't get me wrong, I love him... He's my brother and to be fair he looks out for me like I do him but working with family? Never a good long-term plan.

Trouble is, when you're in a fight for your survival, no one thinks of the effects on those pushed into the very front line, no matter how young they are and no matter how much they are missing a proper childhood. War is war and in the Flux everyone has to do their bit if they show the merest aptitude for the vision.

"Don't I know it. And I won't lose. I never lose," I say.

Because I'm faster, my mind seeks more efficiently and my kill arc is just gorgeous.

"There'll always be someone better. Just a shame for you that it's me, right?"

"In your most pathetic wet dreams, maybe," I say, then I stare at him. "All right, then. Seven you say. Tell me and let's see how many of them are actually mine."

Alyn smiles and my heart sinks. It's that smile that says he knows he's right so I brace myself for the triumphalism and wonder whether to actually listen or begin to rebuild my arc web for the next strikes because sure as shit I'm not letting him beat me. The little shit starts counting off on his fingers.

"Day one, infiltration of the Cocheda Syndicate. Remember… I rearranged three of their Inners, then the Spear-Header about to dissolve your brain. Your efforts with my backing yielded two of their outer ring. You did slightly better on day two when we hit Gorosama and even got to the Axis Major and her second but I got two as well. So that's six-four, right?

"And just now, well, we all know who really hit old Francescorla, don't we?"

"Yeah, me," I say but without conviction.

Alyn laughs. "Don't lie to yourself. I was just that bit faster. He bit my arc, yours came after."

"No one is faster than me," I say.

Alyn shrugs. I know he's right. He knows I know and he also knows I won't ever admit it.

"Three to go for me… A big six for you. Remind me what the winner gets?"

I don't reply. I turn away from his smug face before I put a fist in it. Fact is, I'm seriously regretting the stupid boast that led to the bet. I should have known better than to give him any more incentive and now he's actually threatening my position as One of

Two. Yes, call me a fuckwit but I actually said if he beat me to ten kills in this phase then I'd let him be One of Two for the next. Stupid. Stupid, stupid, stupid.

But, you know, it's me, right? Forgive me but when was I ever bothered about anyone, let alone *him,* getting the better of me out there in the Flux? And he hasn't got there yet.

Alyn has fallen asleep, the exertion of proving his point exhausting him, apparently. Actually, that's unfair, even for Alyn. Out in the Flux, the pressures on minds are intense and draining. More so on the younger ones. But Alyn's resilient so it isn't just the last hour that's caught up with him, it's the last twenty days, one shift on, one shift off.

I should sleep too. This is the calm before the cliché after all. Soon the door will open and the order given to send us back into the Flux. But I can't sleep, so I lever myself out of my moulded recliner and go through a few stretches. Our recliners are side by side and face a wall on which modulating colours, shapes and images are projected. They're supposed to induce relaxation outside the Flux and subliminally concentrate focus within it. Right now they all seem a bit bright and nauseating so I turn my back on them.

Inevitably, my eyes alight on Alyn. When he's asleep, he retains the angelic quality he had when he was a baby. His face is soft and round, his eyelashes gorgeously long and his hair, which he likes to keep neat and tidy, is being riffled by the gentle breeze being piped in from outside where winter has finally given way to the warmth of spring.

A delicate smile is playing about his lips and when he exhales he makes a cooing sound. I really want to be furious with him but I'm not. I mean, it's all my own doing, right? A stupid boast to provoke sibling rivalry. Got more than I bargained for, didn't I? Still, it was nothing more than I'd have done when I was thirteen.

I sit down on the edge of his recliner and he shifts ever-so-slightly. I smooth a stray hair from his face and feel the softness of his skin.

"Just remember that the game isn't the thing, isn't the only thing anyway. And I'll need you out there watching my back just as I'll be watching yours. Don't let the chase deflect you, Little Prince." The tension is easing and I can feel my mind returning to a more stable place. "Just don't do anything dumb, that's all…"

He won't because that's what the real talents are like. They never make mistakes, just do what needs to be done.

"I'll do my best," comes a giggling whisper.

I push myself to my feet. "Have you been awake the whole time?"

Alyn opens one eye. "Why, did I miss something?"

"You little shit," I say but I'm laughing. "How's your head?"

"Still feels a bit… bloated, if you know what I mean. But I'm feeling good."

"If you're really better than me, you'll beat me to ten without trying… understand?"

Alyn grins. "I hear you, Big-Sis."

"Get back to sleep. We may not have much more time."

"You too. And don't worry, when I'm One of Two I'll be the best One of Two. Like you."

I turn away that bit too quickly after I smile at him so he knows I'm welling up. The tone of the music begins to change. The calming melodies begin to scale towards urgency. The scent in the chamber moves from soporific to invigorating and the lighting strengthens by lazy degrees.

"So soon?" says Alyn.

"By my reckoning that's the one point two millionth time you've cracked that joke."

"Once for every minute of my life."

I raise my eyebrows. The bugger's mind is so sharp he's probably right, or near as makes no difference.

"You do not hear the endless repetition in my nightmares."

"No," he agrees. "I have my own."

I nod. None of us escapes the terrors of being lost in the Flux, a mind adrift, vulnerable, calling for help none can give. I'm about to speak some platitude or other when the door slides back and Father walks in. I want to tell you that his face is lined with worry, that his eyes are brim with tears he prays not to spill and that his heart is beating out of his chest with love but I can't.

Alyn scrambles to his feet with a look on his face more akin to a puppy fearing a beating than the son of the man before him. And our father looks at us, appraising our fitness and the looks in our eyes same as he always does. He nods.

"Ready?"

"Yes, Father," says Alyn quickly, desperate to please and with no need to do so. He already has nothing to prove.

I shrug and nod. "Who's the bunny?" I know already, of course.

He looks like he might bite my head off but instead just gives a little sigh. "Cocheda. Reckon you can handle her?"

"Reckon you can be any more off-hand?"

"This is a war," he says as if that explains absolutely everything.

"And owning emotions is a waste of time, is it? We're your children, not your subordinates."

"There's time for all that later," he says, both uncomfortable and cross now.

"Not if we die in about an hour's time. You've really nothing to say to us beyond the mission briefing you're about to delegate?"

"Just don't let me down," he says, after a pause. Sound parenting. "The opco is here with the details. Heed them, this is not going to be easy."

"We'll tear them up, Father," says Alyn. "You'll be proud."

But Father has already turned away and the opco is in the doorway and I barely listen to her drone on about the fulcrum of the axis; and how we're supposed to penetrate it; and what Cocheda's signature will look like; and likely resistance and general opposition levels and all that stuff because she hasn't ever been in the Flux and that means she doesn't have a bloody clue.

"Did you catch any of that?" asks Alyn the moment the severe face has withdrawn and the door is closed.

I shake my head.

"So, the usual routine, then?" he asks.

I nod my head. He smiles.

"Good," he says then his smile falters. "I wish you wouldn't talk to him like that."

"Like what, exactly?"

"Like you're picking a fight."

"I just want him to admit some fatherly feelings towards us. He was a Roamer; he knows what we face."

"He's proud of us, you can see that," said Alyn.

"So's the opco every time we come home, so what? I don't need his acknowledgement that we're good at our job. I need him to admit he cares."

"Of course he cares!" snaps Alyn and his cheeks flush a little.

I remember being like that, defending him to the hilt while he sidestepped affection. I want to snap back, to tell Alyn that Father only cares for his standing and reputation but there's no point. He'll work it out and, anyway, I need Alyn grounded and balanced for what's to come.

"I'm sure he does," I say.

The metronomic pulse is beginning to intrude and the music has faded. The light is bright and warm. The pulse will regulate our hearts inside the Flux and anchor us to our bodies on some subconscious level or other.

"We should settle," says Alyn.

"So we should."

We return to our recliners and I feel the comfort surround me, keeping me light, weightless almost so nothing physical can distract me while I'm in the Flux. Our recliners are connected by a rest on which our arms lie so our hands can touch. It's not standard but it helps us, keeps us locked.

The moment our fingers meet has always been the most magical. I don't know how other Twos do it but in that touch the bonds are broken, our bodies become as memories and our minds are free to travel. That's the easy bit of course, for a Roamer anyway. The hard bit is, well, everything else. I hear the door open behind me. Alyn ripples his fingers against mine.

"You'll never catch me, you know," he says.

"Just watch me. Watch the master at work. I'll have my six before you reach eight."

Alyn laughs because he thinks I'm joking. He's about to discover that I'm not. He's a little tired, you see. And like a horse racing for the line, it's not how you begin, it's how you finish.

"Flux alignment in ten seconds," says our opco from the door. She starts to count down but I don't hear her voice beyond nine. Her world, her tethered limited world is already behind me.

"Come on, Little Prince, let's do some damage."

The Flux aligns, its maw yawns wide and we are sucked into the blistering seething mayhem. We're moving, Alyn and I. All the minds launched into the Flux are and it's like seeing the world drawn in pen and ink, and there's such a wind it smears every mark the pen makes. But within that smear are the shapes and colours of minds. Every mind is there in the Flux. It's where they can be seen.

Your mind is there too. Lucky for you that because your mind is tethered, locked down, and you can't roam, someone like me can't attack you. So I float above you and I pity you and envy you in equal measure.

I always shudder when we move over the front lines. There is so much pain and violence and we can see it all playing out and we can hear locked-down minds howling their fear and their anger at death. Watching a mind flee into oblivion as its body dies is like watching a child throw water on wet paint. Something vibrant, original and alive destroyed in a single off-hand moment.

Moving across the battle lines there are so many deluged this way. We turn our minds from the sheer scale of it, knowing we can end it if we focus now. Cocheda is the fulcrum master, the key stone. Without her the enemy shell will come crashing down. We'll have access to their sanctum and once inside we can rip out every single untethered mind within.

We've struggled so hard to earn the opportunity. Hundreds of Roamers have perished, hundreds more are with us today and it is me and Alyn who have the task. Cocheda knows we are coming for her and she will fight. Lucky I'm so good or we might be in trouble.

"He chose us," says Alyn, because we can speak to one another.

"Don't mistake that for any form of affection," I say, knowing exactly what he's thinking. "We're it because we're the best, no other reason."

"But our victory will make him proud."

"It'll make his legacy. Wise-up, Alyn. And focus; we're over the outers already."

Alyn is upset with me; his emotions are washing over me. He'll settle, he always does, so I leave him to brood.

Below us, we've left the battle lines behind. The ink-washed lands are littered with minds dead and dying. Around us and ahead of us, Roamers are clustered in their formations, anticipating the outer-wave defence. Those who surround us will be trying to open a path right to the fulcrum, no easy task. Others will try to keep enemies from us while we track Cocheda, no easy task.

I can feel the enemy now and in the next instant I can see them too, coalescing out of the wind-blown landscape of smeared-ink buildings and hills and beyond, a chaotic sea. They are spread on a wide front and unafraid. Every mind has its unique meld of colours, tones and shape but the one thing uniting them is a deep grey strand of defiance. Even though we are in the ascendant, their belief in their ability to thwart us is undiminished.

And so it should be. Fighting mind-to-mind is founded so much on confidence and clarity. One slip by either side and the situation could reverse in the next instant.

"Forget them," says Alyn. "Forget all of them. Go where they don't and we'll find our marks. And remember I'm going to kick your arse for ten."

"Of course you are." Whatever gets him into the right space works for me. "Cosy up now, the outriders are in combat."

In the violent silence of the Flux, minds are swirling about each other, colours flaring and mixing. Defence and attack strategies are deployed. Images are projected onto the daubed canvas of the flux, designed to distract. Random memories and detailed fantasies… a laughing child on a swing; the first kiss of lust; a great beast clashes its jaws, splintering feeble bone.

The first arc splits the Flux. It is beautifully formed, a pearlescent hexagonal prism curved over a hundred and twenty or even a hundred and thirty degrees, I reckon. Power and grace and malevolence roll together; the arc snaps across the space between minds. One flares gloriously, the other is simply erased.

I have seen this a thousand times and I pray to see it a thousand more. Any revulsion has long-since diminished to routine even though, in a chamber just like mine, someone has died. I can feel no sorrow; it is a distracting, disabling emotion.

Roamer minds stream past us, breaking off to all points of the compass. I can feel Alyn's desire to be sucked into their slipstream so I hold back. The path is not yet clear. Our Roamers strike hard. Distraction images fill the Flux, arcs crack across the wind-smudged sky and we fly into the space they make. Outriders come to our flanks, surrounding us. We are a globe of minds, a bowling ball racing down the lane to destroy the pins of Cocheda's fulcrum.

The names of those we have picked apart flash in my mind and out into the Flux, taunting her because she can surely see us. There is no hiding our Two, why would we? With signatures as well-known as ours, we are ahead in every battle we join.

"Defensive net," I say. "I'll run distraction."

"Roger, skipper," he says.

"Idiot."

But I love his lack of fear. It's what makes him so gloriously dangerous. No tension, no delay, no mercy.

"Rising, zone five," says Alyn, his voice slightly altered by the concentration of his defensive work which sends pulses into the Flux, disrupting the space on which every arc depends to travel.

I look at my ten o'clock and down. There they are, minds from the fulcrum defence. Not Cocheda, this is just the prelims.

"Seen. Six-up."

"Sector one, direct," says Alyn.

Another cluster at twelve o'clock coming directly at us.

"Seen. Four-up."

The outriders will wait for us to make our move and split accordingly.

"Flux otherwise calm in our district."

"Let's take the six-up," I say. "Sector five. I need six for my ten."

I feel Alyn prickle; perfect. "Spin it, then," he says.

You know that playground game where you hold crossed hands with a partner, lean out and twirl round fast as you dare? Only the skilled don't trip over their feet or lose grip and go flying. We play this game with our minds and we're *very* good at it. We blur, confusing the enemy arcers while we're still able to see and to strike cleanly ourselves. Some trick even though it pisses off some of our roamers, who reckon we're not in control.

How little they know.

We direct ourselves at the six-up. Another Two comes with us, while a second stays on point. The rest split for obs and to attack the four-up.

"Pick your target," I say.

"Done," says Alyn, all focus now.

"Want first try?"

"Why not?"

We tumble towards the six-up. They're throwing distraction to all points. A giant sea creature rears from the smear to grab ay my head. Clumsy. Way, way too obvious. The six minds cluster, the Twos attempting to revolve about one another. Arcs fly from our Roamers and defensive nets shimmer.

Alyn waits, watching. He sees the flat spot that indicates a weakness and he arcs. So accurate. The arc, a simple fifty degree-er, pierces the net, extinguishing a mind. Automatically the net moves, exposes a second mind for an instant. I'm ready. Two down.

Shorn of their others, the broken Twos flee, sucked back towards the dubious sanctuary beneath their fulcrum. The surviving Two heads for the four-up close by, looking to join it. They don't make it.

I feel Alyn's exhilaration. "Eight-five."

"I can count," I say.

There's a multiple flash on my three. We spin closer. Cocheda's forces have struck back hard. Colour trails fade and another six-up rises through them, tones exultant.

"More coming. Zone seven and eight."

"Trying to back door us," I say. "Let's take the new six."

"More than perfect," says Alyn.

"You know nothing can be mo –"

"English lessons? Now?"

I laugh and Alyn laughs with me. We are spinning fast, moving fast. Outriders are with us. I can see the blurred outline of Cocheda's sanctum rising from the shimmering streets of her city that is festooned with the colours of tethered minds. She's close.

The six-up does not shy from us. Outriders move to join us, colours bright and confident. Others move on the flanks, seeking enemies who would thwart the primary mission. Fighting rages across the Flux in an orgy of arc flash, imagery and the dissolution of colours to extinction. With every moment, the intensity increases.

Alyn and I swoop on the six, both preparing pure arcs, both running our shield and distraction routines. Enemy minds shift, colours dilute to weaker tones, fear infects them.

I see an opening, more a chasm, in their net. My arc deluges one mind. Alyn follows, his arc anticipated and blocked but my instant response is not. Eight-seven.

"Getting tired, Little Prince?"

He says nothing and while I lay on as perverse a distraction show as any I have projected in this conflict, he fakes an arc, sees the enemy defence begin to react then goes again, his strike a glorious, one-five-five-er.

"Nine-seven."

Point taken, but there She is and her sheer force sends a ripple through friend and foe alike. Cocheda's mind signature is no bigger than anyone else's but her presence is massive, dwarfing that of her Two who would be the best she possessed.

I feel an ephemeral moment of anxiety. She is on the attack, determined to avenge the killing of Francescorla. No one likes to lose their mentor, not to young Roamers like me and Alyn. She is the last of her syndicate's great minds and she will not go meekly. Into the after-image glare following the thrashing vividity of her distraction imagery come many, many more of her people.

"That's more than a few."

Alyn has always been a master of understatement. Someone back in our sanctum had right royally screwed up and a whole lot of our minds were going to pay the ultimate price.

"Keep going."

"It's going to be a slaughter," says Alyn.

"Not if we take down Cocheda."

"And I only need one for my ten," he says.

"I'll be more than happy if you get her for it. Let's go. Trust the outriders."

We spin towards Cocheda, who is not hiding herself. She moves in a slow elegant helix with her Two while other minds flow about her, moving out to counter the incoming Roamers.

The Flux is inundated with imagery, arcs criss-cross the space. The flash and glare echo and ricochet.

We drive down a narrowing tunnel where Cocheda waits. This is the battle; this is the game right here and where we thought it would be a straightforward strike and return, the mass of minds she has been able to bring to bear mean it will be anything but.

A Two breaks through our Roamers and rushes towards us. Alyn throws up a spectacular distraction; storms suffocate the sky and lightning sheets and forks. In the moment's uncertainty, I snap out an arc and a mind bites it, flaring briefly before fading away. And before the second mind can react, I strike again.

We know the score. "The next one's yours," I say. "You've earned it."

I feel Alyn's surge of pride and of love. "You mean that?"

"Yes," I say. And I do. "You deserve to be a One."

"Thank you," he says and back in the sanctum there will be tears on his face.

"Focus. Remember your ten for the win doesn't have to be Cocheda."

"I hear you."

If the Flux carried sound, we would surely all be deafened. It is like nothing I have ever experienced. Roamers and Cocheda's forces swarm around each other. You can barely see the distraction imagery for the sheer concentration of arcs and the flaring and modulating of defensive shields.

While we plough our furrow, minds on both sides coalesce into blocs, seeking multi-layered defence and overwhelming offensive force simultaneously. Cocheda waits and watches. We drive in faster, spin more quickly, evade any who come at us now and engage.

"Concentrate on your arcing," I say. "I'll do the rest."

"Thank you," says Alyn.

"Just don't screw up." Alyn giggles a little nervously. I link into his shield

We are close and still she waits. She'll let her people do her work for her if they can but she is not afraid of us. I wonder how old she is. She could be young like Alyn or she could be older 'n me. Does she have a dead face or one that lights up when it smiles? I'll never know. Here we meet and one of us will soon be dead because that is the way of my world.

She tries an arc from way out. Speculative, sure, but she's accurate and powerful and I can feel the weight across the shield. We feel it testing and probing but that's all it's meant to do.

"Easy," says Alyn.

"Don't be fooled."

Cocheda attacks again, a concerted series of arcs, long, short and even forked on multiple fronts. I weave the shield tight, anticipating, pushing back, conserving my energy and knowing every strike drains me just that bit more.

"You *can* arc back," I say.

"Waiting my chance," says Alyn. "Don't rush me."

We're spiralling about each other now, our minds seeking weak spots and finding none. I can sense the battles surrounding us and have no option but to trust that our Roamers will hold on long enough to give us the time we need.

Alyn snaps out an arc. Its form is perfect and it launches into a distraction wave I've made but dissipates across their shield. He goes again, this time his arc is long and almost one fifty degrees. It shines with the power he possesses and jumps the gap faster than the brain can follow. Yet it too is caught and rendered harmless, causing only the briefest shimmer in Cocheda's shield.

"They're good," says Alyn.

"So they are," I reply. "Keep going. I'm solid."

It's punch and counter punch. Where most battles are done in one, maybe two arcs, we trade blows like in a boxing bout where neither fighter will take a backward step. It's attrition. Cocheda prefers the multiple jab and body punch style, aiming to grind us down, while Alyn favours the knockout shots, seeking to exploit tiny weaknesses in defence.

Then it happens, I mean it has to, doesn't it? Alyn's and Cocheda's arcs deploy at precisely the same moment and their energies collide with a staggering repulsion force. The feedback sends us spinning away and I can see Cocheda's Two struggling to refocus, their colours running together, their shield flaring and guttering as I knew ours is.

We're vulnerable. My mind is ringing from the backwash of raw arc power and I'm trying to pull the threads of the shield together. Alyn has gone quiet and I wonder if he's conscious but then there is a grunt and a moan and relief floods me.

"Alyn, talk to me."

"I'm shaking I think," he says. "Give me a moment, I'm okay."

"You're not, I can sense it. Your colours are dilute and your voice is unclear. We need to get out of here."

"NO!" The vehemence of his shout takes me aback. "We have to finish this."

I have the shield rebuilt and am throwing out distraction as fast as I can. Cocheda is steady, waiting. This has drained her as well. She's there for the taking but not by us.

"There'll be another time," I say.

"Look at her, she's weak."

"So are we," I say. "So are you. Admit it."

"Father gave us this task. I'm not running away and neither are you."

There has been a pause in the battle across the Flux. Every mind has felt the shock of the collision, sought its source and assessed its impact. A sick sensation crawls across me. Never mind Cocheda, every enemy Two is eyeing us up. Our Roamers get back into the fight, sensing the problem but I can sense the shift in confidence. We're weaker than Cocheda.

"Spin up," I say. "We need to move."

"Ahead not backwards."

We start to spin and I can feel the energy returning but Alyn is slow.

"Look at her shield," says Alyn as we spin back in. "Tattered. Easy pickings."

And it is but caution is screaming at me. Cocheda sees us moving and their colours brighten, their shield beginning to knit but slowly. I catch my breath.

"This is our chance," says Alyn and there's strength in his voice again.

"Honestly. How much do you have left?"

"Not much. Couple of arcs. Enough."

The sentiment across the Flux shifts again. Our Roamers have seen us spin back into the fight and their defences harden, their colours brighten and they push back. We spin around Cocheda's Two whose movement is sluggish. Their shield is incomplete. Alyn is trying to draw me in to strike now.

"It's a trap," I say. "Wait."

"It's our chance," says Alyn. "We can make Father proud and we can do it now."

"Don't do it for him, do it for us. We're the Two, we make the choice. Pick your moment, guard your mind."

"Come on!"

His pull on our spin is driven by the glory he can all but touch. I flood the Flux with distraction and weave as many frequencies into my shield meld with Alyn as I can. His focus is imperfect and I know I have to remain at peak clarity.

"Be careful, Little Prince. I can't do this without you."

His love floods our Two. I accelerate our spin and we flash in towards Cocheda. Their shield trembles, they know what's coming but yet they don't try to flee. Alyn is forming his arc and I can feel the energy. He's pouring everything into it, going for the one devastating hit.

"Don't leave yourself dry."

"You'll see me home."

My heart pounds so hard and I know back in my body I'm gasping in breaths. We scorch in and I'm scouring Cocheda for any hint of foul play but there's nothing. Her Two is damaged, minds surely scrambled by the force of the feedback, shield guttering and sparking, feeble distractions flickering.

Alyn's arc snaps across the space. It is perfection, its hexagonal form a good one-seven-five degrees and glittering with its power. The arc hammers into the guttering shield and blows it apa – no… no it doesn't and in that briefest of times I see it all. I see their shield slam shut on the arc and Cocheda's response feed out so quickly it all but defies the senses. It pierces the ephemeral space left by Alyn's arc and sends a shockwave of enormous magnitude through our shield.

Alyn cries out and his colours shift madly. I feel the weight of his barely conscious mind on mine. But at least he's still alive. Back in our fulcrum, I'll try to comprehend what Cocheda has done, *how* she did it.

"Alyn. Alyn! We're leaving. You're drained, we're done." I'm already pulling us clear.

"I can get her. I can't fail him. I won't fail him."

"You won't fail. It doesn't have to be now."

"It does. The game is here."

He arcs again, a sudden outpouring of power. But it is unfocused, the shape barely conceived. Cocheda's Two bat it aside and her response is brutal, accurate and pure, just as mine would have been in her place. I try to cling on to Alyn but his colours pale and are washed away into the Flux.

I flee at the speed of my screams.

I'm still hugging my brother, my lionhearted brother with his face still damp with those tears of joy, when the door opens and Father walks in. I know it's him by the rhythm of his shoes on the polished tiles.

"What happened?"

I hug Alyn harder, one hand pressing his face to my shoulder, the other around his back. I am praying that he will jerk back to life, that this is all some horrible prank. I can almost believe it is… I would believe it is had I not seen his mind wash away into the Flux.

"What happened?" he asks again, irritation in his tone.

"Alyn is dead," I manage, every word choked out.

"That much is clear. How did it happen?"

I glance at him standing there, his face severe and the knowledge of the failure of his command radiating from the tension in his body. I lay Alyn's body down on to his couch and take one of his still warm hands in mine as I stand. I find I am calm and that I have no need to rage, nor even to raise my voice.

"It happened because he mistook respect for love. It happened because he mistook victory for pride. It happened because he was still young and naïve enough to believe you actually cared about him. But we know the truth don't we, Father? We know why you wanted us."

"Your emotions are muddling your thoughts," he says. "I will return when you are calmer."

"No you will not," I say. "You will not live your failures as a Roamer through me. You will not give me another Two of Two so you can sacrifice me on the altar of your desire for advancement. She is coming for me and I will not stop her but there is something I will do."

"And what is that?" he says, half turning away; done with me now I will be of no more use to him.

I clutch Alyn's hand a little more tightly and my arc snaps out and drills into Father's unguarded mind. For the first time in my life I see his face soften. He crumples.

"Ten," I say. "We win, Alyn. We win."

Twisted Limerick 7

Ramsey Campbell

You may think that some people are odd
For urging you never to nod.
But don't fall asleep,
For upon you will creep
Your simulacrum popped from a pod.

Do You Believe In Ghosts?

Mark West

Having lost Carole Duffin once before, I was determined it wouldn't happen again...

The funeral took place on a wet Thursday afternoon, the mourners huddling under black umbrellas as if repelling an attack. I stood with a couple of old school friends, listening to the rattle of the drizzle over my head, trying but failing to catch the vicar's words.

Although I'd known Carole for over thirty years and we'd been boyfriend and girlfriend in the Sixth Form at Gaffney Tech, our current relationship was only a few months old. She'd divorced her husband due to his insistence on getting other women pregnant, though I could see him standing beside the open grave, tears and rain water running down his cheeks. My own marriage had also fallen apart, work pressures tearing into a bond that I once thought unbreakable. It had been acrimonious and unpleasant, the worst six months of my life and I seriously doubted my ex-wife would have been standing at my graveside crying.

Three months, two weeks and a handful of days. A chance encounter on Facebook led to late night messages, an understanding of the emotional landscape and then a tentative meeting, exchanging pleasantries over the clatter of cutlery and crockery at the café. A realisation that we could make this happen, and suddenly I was a teenager again, asking if she'd like to go on a date. A meal at the local Italian, a trip to the cinema, holding hands on the back row and, later, a kiss in the car as I dropped her off. Things seemed to speed up after that and we spent as much time together as possible, making love as if trying to make up for lost time.

I was the happiest I'd been in years and Carole told me she felt the same. We'd been brought down by divorce but had found each other again in the process and things were going to be different this time.

We'd had a lovely evening. She came to my flat, I cooked spaghetti and made garlic bread, we listened to 80s music and laughed, danced in the kitchen and made love. Normally she'd have stayed over but as she had an early meeting we dozed in each other's arms before she got up at 2 am and left. I waved her off from my window – we blew kisses and promised to phone the next day. I never saw her again.

I didn't know anything was wrong until the following midday when she didn't answer her phone. I rang, on and off, until the early evening and when I still didn't get an answer, I went to her flat. Her friend Annie answered the door, her eyes red and puffy from too many tears.

"Oh Martin," she said and began sobbing, pulling me into a hard embrace, "you were on my list to ring, but I didn't know what to say to you."

"About what? What's wrong, Annie?"

"It's Carole. Last night, a drunk driver."

"She wasn't drunk, she hadn't..." I stopped and prised myself away from Annie, holding her shoulders. "Where is she?"

Annie took in a deep, hitching breath and silent tears rolled down her cheeks. "She's gone, Martin."

I filled my days with work and ploughed headlong into projects that had been languishing in my in-tray for weeks. My boss, the only colleague I'd shared the news with, kept advising me to take things easy but I could see that wasn't going to work. I needed to keep busy, to have my mind filled with something – anything – because the quiet moments let thoughts of Carole creep into my head. I could see our relationship going forward, I could see the many happy years we were due to have together, I could almost hear the sound of her laughter when I caught her unawares with a joke. I could hear the sigh of her breath as I touched her – I could hear her say my name.

Home was the hardest, that small flat she'd never spent more than a couple of nights in at a time, but which seemed to hide traces of her in every corner. A week went by before I realised she'd put a nail care kit into the bathroom cupboard and I sat at the kitchen table for ten minutes, turning it over in my hands.

My friends were sympathetic but we were all in our mid-forties, they had their own families and commitments so the option of going out for a drink, or of playing a few frames of pool or even going for a walk, didn't crop up as often as I'd have liked.

The worst time was when the clock ticked past midnight, heralding the long hours before dawn. Two days after I found the nail care kit, I went online and found a handful of forums for bereaved partners.

I read a lot. People claiming to be psychic were all over the threads like a rash, promising to speak to loved ones for a small financial compensation and, even in my mind-state, it disgusted me. There were exhortations to accept Jesus into my heart, detailed examinations of happy lives that had been ripped asunder, too many tales of people contemplating ending their own lives, all of them interspersed with spam for sunglasses and Viagra. One forum seemed to consist of recently widowed women in their fifties who, realising they still had a libido to satisfy, would be willing to entertain gentlemen callers on a non-exclusive basis. I didn't look at the mirror forum for men still looking for sex.

I developed an introductory biography to use if people on the forums – which were very busy late at night – asked. Mine read: *'Bereaved boyfriend. Knew my partner for 30+ years, went out whilst at school, only re-connected recently. Taken away in a car accident. Feel very lonely."* The responses I got were generally good, apart from the desperate women who wanted to meet me for sex, but nothing really connected to what I felt because I didn't quite know what I wanted – or expected – to happen. I knew nobody could wave a magic wand and bring her back. I knew I couldn't travel back in time and insist she stay overnight, with promises that I would get her up bright and early for her meeting. I didn't want my guilt assuaged, that wasn't the point.

The forum pages filled quickly. People started random threads for pretty much anything – what they'd just seen on TV, what was on sale at Asda, which advert they liked – and most had the views to show how niche they were.

Five pages in, I came to a thread, dated a fortnight ago, that caught my eye and the simplicity of its title stopped me: *"Do you believe in ghosts?"*

Of course I didn't. I live in the real world and I've had enough people depart from my life to know that if there was anything beyond this mortal coil, I'd have seen it. Fourteen people had already viewed this thread. I was fifteenth.

The first post, added by the thread originator who called himself Hector Sebastien, read *"Simple question – do you believe or not? Leave a comment"*

Two of the comments were for sunglasses, one was from a woman who declared that the thread was the work of the devil (I assumed she'd answered yes) and half of the others were a curt "NO!" Another couple had considered responses, where the author had clearly been working through something in their own mind. I decided to add my own.

GRIEVING46: *I would say no, purely because I've never seen one (yet have had people from my own life pass away). Having said that, right now I would gladly say yes if I could see my girlfriend again.*

I re-read my comment several times, my mouse pointer hovering over the Post button. "Ah," I said, "who cares?" and clicked. The thread updated, I came out and scrolled for another hour or so before giving up and going to bed. Where I lay for a long time in the darkness, listening to the house settle around me and the sound of my own breathing.

The next morning, sitting in the lounge with a bowl of cornflakes on my lap and a cup of tea steaming on the windowsill, I checked my email. One of them was from the grief forum.

HECTOR SEBASTIEN: Thank you for your post, GRIEVING46, I believe you and want to help you. Are you interested?

I finished my cereal. What did he mean? The last thing I needed now was to attract the attention of some nutter who believed he could commune with the dead. But – and I couldn't quite put my finger on why – that wasn't the impression I got from the post. I put my bowl on the floor, retrieved my laptop from its bag and booted it up. I went straight to the forum and found the post.

GRIEVING46: I am very interested, but also very sceptical and not in the mood for games. The first mention of psychic ability and/ or payment and we're done.

I went for a shower and by the time I got back, there was another post.

HECTOR: This is not a game, I am not psychic and I do not want any money.

The post was three minutes old and his icon still registered as online.

I bit my lip, thinking of the best response. I couldn't see his angle, what kind of trick was this? And even as I thought that, I wondered about the logic if it wasn't a trick. What if there was something, even if it was only the great and overwhelming need of the bereaved to be shown the light for just a moment or two? The world is full of weird stories, of odd and unusual things happening to people at times of great stress. What if he could tell me something, some manipulation of time or logic that would let me see Carole again? I didn't believe in ghosts, I really didn't, but I'd be willing to believe in anything if it meant I could see her again.

GRIEVING46: Then I'm interested.

HECTOR: Good. So if you could see your loved one again, even if only for five seconds, would you do it?

I answered without thinking.

GRIEVING46: Yes.

HECTOR: I have to go to work now, but I will contact you this evening, if that's okay?

I watched his icon status switch to offline.

The day went by in a blur, my thinking dominated by what Hector Sebastien might know or be able to tell me. I messed up a management report and only just caught my error before I sent it out. I must have had enough of a distracted air for a couple of people to ask if I was okay, then glance guiltily at their feet when I looked at them with wide and confused eyes.

I battled the rush hour traffic, yelled at more drivers than usual and got home a little before six. I checked my email – nothing – and went straight to the forum. There were no new posts by Hector, who still showed as offline and no messages in my inbox. I paced around my lounge, got changed, checked my email, made a sandwich, checked the forum, ate my sandwich.

He came online at seven. My forum Inbox pinged at seven-ten.

HECTOR: Hello GRIEVING46, sorry for the delay, I got caught up in traffic. Are you ready?

GRIEVING46: Yes, of course.

HECTOR: Okay, you don't know me and this all sounds ridiculous (I know, it did to me) but it does work. No gimmicks, no crap and you don't have to pay anything. What this does involve, however, is a little ritual. Do you have a problem with that, because if you do we can't go on.

A ritual? Well, unless he was going to ask me to strip naked and film myself on the webcam, I didn't see that it could hurt.

GRIEVING46: So long as there's no sacrifice, yes I'll do a ritual.

HECTOR: Okay, follow this list and there won't be any problems. You'll need a photograph of you and the deceased but it needs to be on proper, old-school photographic paper. Not the crap you get from supermarkets these days and certainly not something you've printed out on A4

GRIEVING46: Does it have to be an old photograph?

HECTOR: Yes. You're looking to get an image that was bonded as part of the process, taken
directly from the latent image. I don't know why that's so important but it is. The rest sounds like
a bad movie but you need something of the deceased, hair is preferable and something of yourself,
hair or skin. On the night of a full moon, put the items on the photograph and set fire to it. If
you've used an old photograph, it should curl around the items so they all burn together. Say this

incantation: "Exaudi me, quaeso, misericordia reducam ad te" until the photograph is dust.

That didn't seem like too much of a problem. I looked out of the window. The sun was going down, the room growing dull.

GRIEVING46: But if this does work, why doesn't everyone do it?

HECTOR: Because not everyone knows. Do it for yourself then pay it forward to one person and
one person only.

I couldn't work out the angle. If he was going to have a laugh at me, for burning an old photograph, how would he ever know?

GRIEVING46: I don't understand.

HECTOR: Of course you don't but fulfil this ritual and you will have your desire.

GRIEVING46: Thank you for sharing with me.

HECTOR: Goodbye, GRIEVING46.

His icon went dull and I blew out my breath, my heart thumping. I knew the ritual had to be fake but that didn't stop the frisson of excitement that ran through me. I checked Google and saw a full moon was due in three days. I could wait for that.

I went into Google translate and typed in the incantation Hector had given me. *Hear my desire, I pray to you to bring back my loved one.*

I checked the forums the next morning before I went to work and later into the night, but didn't see any more posts from Hector Sebastien. The rational part of me knew that what he'd written was rubbish – all I'd be doing was destroying an old photograph – but at the same time I wanted, I *needed* to believe. I knew I would do it.

Whenever my mind wandered at work, I imagined myself in the kitchen starting the fire and waiting patiently, listening intently. I imagined Carole would come to the kitchen, draping herself theatrically around the door jamb.

"Hello lover," she would say and smile that smile and I would melt into her and she into me.

That evening, I sat on my bed with a box-folder of old photographs I'd been intending to sort into albums for years. Inside was a riot of colourful paper envelopes with company names I hadn't seen or thought of in ages. I sifted through them, opening packs at random and seeing faces and places long removed from today, and the process took longer than I thought it would. Most of the Carole pictures were in a Truprint wallet, dating back to the mid-80s and I looked at the pair of us, so in love in our mid-teens. I was handsome, with a thick mop of dark hair, skinny arms and a thing for drainpipe trousers. Carole looked even prettier than I remembered, in cardigans and pastel-coloured shirts, with permed (sometimes spiky) hair and a lot of eye make-up. I could see, staring at our faces preserved in the photo emulsion, that we were meant for each other, it was all too clear in our expressions.

I found a picture that made me smile. I was standing in front of the Sixth Form common room, wearing white trousers and shoes and a pale blue shirt. Carole, in a black cardigan and knee-length white skirt, was draped across my outstretched arms, her head back, smiling broadly.

I photocopied the picture at work the next day. I checked the forum several times and Hector Sebastien was still marked as offline. I re-read our correspondence which became less silly the more I did so.

I was ready before dusk fell, with everything assembled in front of my bedroom window. I took some hair from the brush she'd left in my bathroom and snipped some of my own off with nail scissors. I put them on a plate, on top of the photograph, and laid a box of matches on the floor beside it. I wasn't hungry, but made myself some toast and forced it down with a big glass of wine.

I was sure I believed, I wanted to believe and there was nobody to argue the point. Re-reading the correspondence helped but I thought alcohol would keep me in the mindset so I finished the glass and re-filled it.

I sat cross-legged on the floor, staring through the window at the ever darkening sky. The moon, low and fat, peeked over the houses that backed onto mine. From outside came the normal sounds of a neighbourhood, noises you hear every evening in the summer and barely pay attention too. I drank some more wine and watched the moon rise gradually above the rooftops.

Dusk gave way to twilight, which slowly gave the day to the night. The sounds outside petered away to silence. The bedroom grew dark, the moon painting a rhomboid shape on the carpet. The house was quiet.

"Okay Carole," I said as I slid the plate into the wash of light. The photograph reflected the moon back at me and suddenly I felt silly again, but forced the sensation down.

"Please let this work," I whispered, and struck a match. I blinked but the flare had already imprinted on my retinas. When I opened my eyes again, the flame cast a dancing glow on the picture, the teen-aged us frolicking anew in the Sixth Form block.

I put the match to one corner of the picture but it didn't catch straight away. I watched as the flame licked at the edge, investigating the emulsion. When it finally caught, I shook the match out, put the deadhead on top of the box and watched the photograph succumb to the fire.

The top right corner, now completely black, curled inwards and touched against one of Carole's hairs, which crackled. The flames must have moved under the photo as the middle section darkened and I could now smell the hair burning.

I looked up at the moon.

"Exaudi me, quaeso, misericordia reducam ad te," I said, not sure if I was pronouncing the words correctly or not. I repeated the phrase twice then looked at the plate. The photograph was curling into a cylindrical shape, the outer edges thin and wispy. The hairs were consumed in the flames and smelled horrible.

"Exaudi me, quaeso, misericordia reducam ad te," I said, staring at teen-aged Carole's face until the flames took her from me. I repeated the incantation until the photograph was a black dusty tube on the plate, then looked back at the moon.

Nothing had changed.

I turned, glancing around the room over my shoulder. There was nothing there that hadn't been before I started the ritual and I could feel a flare of anger, deep in my belly. I'd been had, it was fake, a sick joke and I was annoyed at myself for falling for it. I drained the last of my glass, stood up, waited for the kinks to work their way out of my legs and went into the hallway, meaning to go and get a new bottle.

There was a blue-tinged light in the front room, as if the TV had come on. The curtains were open but this wasn't the glow of streetlights. Carefully, my left hand sliding along the wall, my right gripping the wine glass, I walked along the landing. The flat remained silent. I paused at the doorway, then poked my head around.

Something was on the sofa, a blue-grey translucent shape that ebbed and flowed like smoke. I stared, trying to see what was behind it. The shape moved, branches forming and pushing out two below, two at the sides and the top moulded into a rounder shape.

I walked into the room, eyes wide, as hopeful as I was disbelieving. I made my way to the sofa carefully, never taking my eyes from the shape, which became more defined the closer I got. I thought I could see eyes, Carole's eyes. Yes, there was her nose, her lips, the little dimple on her chin. The offshoots slowly became arms and legs, the feet filling out and touching the carpet. Hair began to form, those gentle blonde curves reaching for her shoulders and beyond.

"Carole?" How could this be? "Carole, it's me…"

The shape of Carole didn't acknowledge me but one arm drew out in front of her. The body moved slightly to the left, the other arm reaching towards the sofa cushion. I knelt in front of her, tears running down my cheeks.

"Carole?" She grew more substantial by the second. I could see her eyelashes, the little nick in her left cheek where a childhood incident had been badly stitched. As more of the smoke dissipated, I could see she wore the clothes I'd last seen her in – jeans, with a blue and white striped top. She turned her head and I thought she was looking at me but no, when I smiled, she looked away.

Her right arm moved and as the smoke faded and she became more real, I realised I was watching her driving. And clearly reaching for something.

The image flared, for the quickest of moments, a brightness that brought such clarity to her she could have been real. She smiled, looking ahead. Her arm moved and she leaned to the left, looking towards the sofa cushion. She pulled herself up quickly, startled and put both hands in front of her face, fingers curling.

Her scream startled me, raising goosebumps on my arms.

She jolted, her entire upper body shunted forward, then back just as quickly and her head whiplashed so hard she was looking at her lap, then at the ceiling.

The scream died and as her head settled on her left shoulder, her eyes blank and glassy, so did she.

I knew what five seconds Hector Sebastien had gifted me.

Another flare and the scene repeated itself. I clasped my hands over my ears but that made no difference, as if the sound were trapped inside my head. I ran downstairs to the street but could still hear her, though the darkened windows around me suggested no-one else did.

I went back upstairs, my mind a jumble, trying to form a coherent thought. I grabbed the laptop and went into the forum but there was no profile for Hector Sebastien, no thread, no trace the man had ever been there at all. As I looked and clicked and read, Carole's terrifying scream accompanied me, sending cold spears up my back and into the base of my skull and turning my stomach every time. The thought that a heart-shredding scream had been her last moment was almost too much to bear.

I kept coming back to why he'd chosen me, why he'd done this – had I responded in a certain way and, if that was the case, had someone done the same to him?

Pay it forward, he'd written. To one person only.

I took my hands from my ears and sat at the table in front of the laptop. I opened a new thread on the forum, my typing punctuated by Carole's screams, each one of which drove shards of pain into my head. I wrote the title of the thread, then the body of the post and pressed enter.

It took a moment or two to appear on screen.

"Do you believe in ghosts?"

Twisted Limerick 8

Ramsey Campbell

At first you may think he's a crank,
The chap who maintains that he shrank.
But each time he's seen
He's more short and more lean,
Till where he had been is a blank

The Loathing of Strangers

Sarah Pinborough

"We're sorry to announce that the 08.34 Virgin Intercity to London Euston has been delayed by approximately twenty five minutes. This is due to an earlier signal failure at Watford Junction."

The winter breeze does little to blow away the growing sense of irritation around me. People check their watches as if this will somehow hurry along the missing train. More passengers drift down the stairs and emerge from the lift, faces falling at the realisation that they probably have no chance of a seat. There is no *right* time of day for a delayed train, but this is definitely the wrong one.

The platform isn't crowded but is inching towards heavily-populated. That suits me. It's easy to be anonymous in busy places. "Third time this week," the commuter to my left mutters to everyone and no one. I ignore him. My eyes are fixed elsewhere. On the person I've followed. The man whose routine has become my own in recent weeks.

He's standing beyond the yellow line – well into the disallowed no man's land.

Suicide by train must be only for those utterly consumed by self-loathing. What faster way is there to make thousands of strangers the length of the country loathe you within minutes of your death. *A fatality on the line.* The words all train travellers dread coming over the tannoy. The words that within minutes cause vitriol to be poured onto the recently departed, before the remnants of their flesh and bone, dragged far up tracks, have even cooled. *Selfish fucker. Retarded thoughtless idiot. Why couldn't the useless shit have just taken some pills? Why screw up everyone else's day?*

No, suicide by train is not for those who have any sense of

tragedy about themselves. To be hated by strangers simply for finding the world too much to cope with, now that really is rock bottom, whatever the therapists say.

What must it feel like? That moment in midair before the speeding metal hits. Does everything stop? Is there time for regrets? A wish to take that final step *back*? What do you hear last? I answer my own rhetorical question instantly. The screeching of brakes. Squealing metal. I know it only too well.

For a while, *after*, that high-pitched squeal was all I could hear. That and the inevitable awful crunching that followed. I'm not supposed to think of these things. They're a trigger, apparently. Even ten years and so much counselling on, the triggers remain. Anything metallic can do it on a bad day. I tell people I choose not to drive. That I don't need a car. Whether they believe me or not is up to them. I say it in such a way there is no invitation to discussion, and those few left close enough to me to try, my ageing parents, my brother and his wife, long ago stopped trying to dig deeper. They can't possibly understand.

Platform 10, ten years on from when a ten-year-old smiling tomboy girl-child and her mother died. My teeth clench with the ever-present memory of the awful crunch of panels crumpling. The copper tang of blood in my mouth, nose numb from smashing against the steering wheel. Ten years on and the planets have aligned. Here we are.

Drunk driver.

He's looking at his feet. His hair has thinned since I was last this close to him. He looks older, much as I do myself. Prematurely aged. I went grey nearly overnight. I'm still ashen-skinned. He looks hollowed out. Does he remain broken? Cowed? Or is this just the way he stands by nature, slouched and untidy. I can't decide if his suit is hanging loose on him because he's lost weight, or if it's designed to be that way. I used to be so on top of fashion. Not any more.

More people fill the platform and I move closer, my heart racing. I stay the right side of the line. I don't want him to see me.

Would he recognise me now? Probably, just as I would forever know him. Some faces you can't forget, however much you might wish too.

"Please stand back from the platform edge, the next train at platform ten does not stop here."

The idea began to grow in me last summer after that spate of horrendous news stories. The random hate-filled crimes where unsuspecting innocents took the brunt. The Sikh man pushed in front of a tube train by some drunk BNPer shouting about how *the Muslims started it*. There were four more deaths after that, and the one which stuck in my head most was where the man in question had been scrabbling frantically to get back up on the platform when the train hit. His *moment* lasted longer than most. How much awful disbelief must he have felt.

I couldn't stop thinking about it. I'd had that kind of disbelief before. The kind you feel only in situations where a random moment has changed everything. One moment that has ended lives. Five minutes earlier or five minutes later and it could all have been different. Sliding doors. It's the sort of thinking that drives a person mad. Perhaps I have gone mad. I think I have. But sanity or otherwise, that was when I started to formulate my plan.

A good push could leave someone in the middle of the tracks. Stunned for a second. Just enough time to realise what was about to happen, to panic, before being pulped into oblivion.

Is it too much for him? Should I turn and walk away? It's a ridiculous thought. I haven't come this far to change my mind now. I need to be free. I've endured ten long years of him. His very continuing existence has kept me imprisoned, trapped in that moment, unable to move on. He is the cockroach in my head. He's everywhere I look. I see him in my nightmares, in the faces of strangers on the street, sometimes I even see him when I look in the mirror. He's become so much a part of me I don't know where I end and he begins, but if I am ever to feel anything resembling life again, then this man in front of me has to die.

I see the headlights of the train shimmering in the cold sunlight further down the track. The eyes of a sleek metal snake powering towards us. Tonnes of steel. These panels won't crumple.

Everyone else around us fades away. The sky is bright. My hands don't feel like my own as I raise them. The wind whips up with the approaching train. I step forward, well across the yellow line, quick and powerful, and shove him hard.

"Hey!"

A hand behind is trying to grab me and I'm so intent in watching *him* tumble to the gravelly tracks below, his eyes wide with surprise, that in my shock I spin round and back away. My feet find only air. My mouth opens in horror, *no no no no not me*, and my arms windmill as I fall, desperate to reach someone, *anyone*, to pull me back to safety. I'm too far out though. The impact of the ground judders through my bones.

Above us, the people on the platform recede like an ocean in the onset of a tsunami.

"Help me!" I say, trying to get to my feet, to scrabble my way to safety.

"You." The voice behind me.

Him.

He grabs my arm and pulls me back, strong for a broken man, forcing me to face him. His eyes are bloodshot. Like mine.

"I was going to jump anyway," he says, his lips twitching into an almost smile.

"Let me go."

I can't breathe. My words are a whisper that wants to be a wail. I was right. The moment we have left is long. Long but not long enough. Not a lifetime long.

It all flashes before me.

The vodka martinis at the party. Driving so fast through those country lanes laughing at my own brilliant youth, my perfect destiny, the luck I had to be born who I was. The drunken euphoria of it all.

The car that came out of nowhere.

My breath holds as we stare at each other. No lies. Not now.

Not out of nowhere.

It came round the bend. I was on the wrong side of the narrow road.

"You don't get to walk away this time." His eyes shine with victory. He looks more alive than he has in all the time I've known him.

I've never known him. I ran from knowing him.

Why couldn't he have died with them? My father made sure I didn't have to go to prison – a faulty light on the grieving father's car, the results of my breathalyser being contaminated, the old boy network making sure one foolish moment didn't destroy my entire life. But of course it did. Guilt is not so easy to rub out as the truth. *He* was always there. This broken handsome man. The poster boy for drink driving adverts – *"Don't make someone else feel this pain".* How could I ever be free while he was alive? His face as I walked free from court. My waking thought for ten years. His face behind my eyes. The disgust. The pain. A ten year old girl mirrored in them.

Somewhere on the platform a woman screams. I want to break free and scramble for the edge, but it's too late. It's always been too late.

I can hear it. The screeching of metal as the driver desperately tries to slow down.

I didn't even try to slow down.

I feel sorry for the train driver. Two men locked together in a fate, about to become three. We will forever be a part of him. I feel sorry for the people on the platform.

I feel sorry for myself.

It's what I do best.

He had crying by the side of the road, a broken arm hanging useless as he stared at the wreck of the car in the verge, only the driver's side relatively undamaged. His wife and child and the crumpled panels and the bark of the solid country tree, had become one. Flesh, wood and steel. A terrible hybrid.

I stood further away. A broken nose. The taste of rust in my mouth. Watching. Disbelief. My fault. Can't be my fault. Why were they out this late? Why would a family be out this late? I did not go to him. I could not be contaminated by his grief. This did not belong in my life.

I called my father. Help me, Dad, I've done something stupid.

Something stupid.

Not something stupid. Something terrible.

I was right about the moment. It does stop. For long enough for everything to become clear. I am afraid. I am panicking. I am also, surprisingly, something else. I am tired. I am tired of me. I am tired of *that* moment.

"I'm sorry," I whisper to him. "I'm so sorry."

He's still gripping my arm and I grip him back with my free hand. We will end this together.

His mouth moves but I don't know if he's giving me absolution or sending me to hell. I can't hear his words over the roar of our impending deaths.

I close my eyes.

And wait for the loathing of strangers.

Twisted Limerick 9

Ramsey Campbell

You may think he's just venting his spleen,
That uncommonly unshaven teen.
But he's not just jejune,
For he's changed by the moon
And grows fur besides fangs that are keen.

The Marble Orchard

Andrew Hook

A shiver of sunlight sparked the trees as though thirsty for illumination. Ronson bit into his butter-soaked toast, savouring the texture. Leaning against his office door – as he did every sunrise; his legs crossed at the ankle – he contemplated the graveyard, where shadows revealed themselves as granite. The curvature of headstones mimicked the dome of the sun on the horizon, although that view was blockaded by rows of houses, high-rises, and skyscrapers which dominated the London landscape. Yet Ronson knew it was there. And the sky would brighten. And once the graveyard was fully immersed in light Ronson would reach over to the table for his cup of tea only to find it had turned cold. As it did, always.

He stepped inside to brew another.

In Ronson's considered opinion, sunrise illustrated the cemetery as its best, which was why he made certain – barring holidays – to arrive in time to witness it. When it came to organising his day he was his own man. His employers were relaxed as to whether he arrived at four am in the summer months or much later during winter. Ronson knew there was an analogy to be had in the rising of the sun over the land of the dead, and that for some people the sun*set* would stir their emotions, but he didn't concern himself much with the theory. Put simply, the light was purer in the morning, unsullied by the pollution which rose skyward during the heat of the day. Ronson grounded himself in reality. Like hospital workers, or morticians, or funeral directors he saw enough of death to understand it was nothing mystical. He was numbed to sensations of the tragic. Maybe this distance was a by-product of his work, although more likely he had chosen this occupation because he was already predisposed to detachment.

He flicked through the local newspaper as he drank his second cup of tea. There was news about the recent developments, of course. Each media outlet had balanced outrage with understanding in an attempt to attract a wide spectrum of potential readers. Few could argue that cemeteries were becoming increasingly full. It was an obvious fact that people died and people would continue to die. There wasn't much room for negotiation. Yet for many years successive governments had fluffed the issue of what to do about it. Space was at a premium in London, no less so in the cemeteries. And people wanted – *needed* – to be buried where they lived. The alternative – cremation – wasn't always appropriate.

Despite the balance in the article, the local paper had taken the line of hyperbole with the headline: *Graves To Be Decimated At Bounds Green Cemetery*. Ronson had to admire the knowing duplicity. The paper was well aware that 10% of graves were targeted under the new legislation, but their average reader's interpretation of *decimated* wouldn't be so literal. At Bounds Green there were upwards of 20,000 plots, meaning Ronson had the initial task of identifying 2000 graves for either *lift and re-inter* or *lift and deepen* purposes. It was no small feat.

He drained the last of his tea, the residue tasting milkier due to the temperature decrease rather than any difference in density of water and milk. The paper quoted a government source which was accurate if not entirely adequate:

A spokeswoman for the council said: "The majority of graves under consideration will be between 100 and 150 years old. Although the burial registers will contain details of who is buried in each grave there will not be any record of the next of kin as they are common graves – they were never purchased, so no ownership records would have been recorded and the graves belong to the council."

Ronson closed the newspaper and folded it. He remembered something on television demonstrating that no piece of paper –

regardless of size – could be folded more than eight times. As he stood and once again regarded the cemetery from his position in the doorway he knew there was a finite amount of times graves could also be *folded* and re-used. He couldn't help but raise a half-smile at the analogy. What would happen when they *really* ran out of space?

Everyday management of the cemetery was – to a certain extent – left to Ronson's discretion. His duties encompassed caretaker, foreman, sympathiser, administrator, and security guard dependent on whether he was opening/closing, supervising gravediggers, offering condolences, sorting paperwork, or kicking out undesirables. The cemetery itself held no crematorium and the arrangements of religious services were out of his remit. Ronson liked it that way. He made it his business to stay out of religion and politics, which was why the new legislation bothered him. For the past week his role had been dominated by affixing small green triangles with cable ties to the headstones of graves he identified as *obsolete*. The word wasn't his, and as with *decimate* it was loaded with meaning. Ronson had found himself grumbling as he worked, and despite his best efforts his mood resembled thunder heralding a storm.

An unseasonably late spring gave an edge to those tasks. Ronson had begun to long for mornings where his breath couldn't be seen leaving his mouth. The winter had been mild in terms of snowfall or rain, but the cold had bitten and continued to bite. Cemeteries were places for quiet contemplation, but with the weather as it was most visitors were swiftly in and out. It was the difference between visiting a prostitute or a mistress. Ronson preferred days where lingering was preferable, more respectful.

His bicycle squeaked as he made his rounds. Cold stiffened his fingers through his gloves. On grassy banks, purple crocuses and mini-daffodils had begun the process of flourishing. Rabbits and squirrels were occasional movements in the peripheries of his vision. The cemetery attracted a variety of birds: the usual sparrows, starlings and blackbirds, but occasionally a woodpecker or a jay. It wouldn't be long before the colours of the trees were in his eyes. Perhaps another couple of weeks and the weather would make an unstoppable change. Ronson would be grateful that the seasonal rebirth could happen here, providing a form of catharsis.

He rounded a corner and rested his bicycle against an oak. A new plot was being dug in the remaining clear cemetery space. He knew the workers, Dave and Jonas. They looked up as he approached. Dave was knee-deep in soft earth, whilst Jonas leant on his spade. They needed to take turns to avoid hitting each other.

The usual nods and pleasantries were exchanged. Dave wiped sweat from his forehead with the back of a glove, leaving a mark of dirt which resembled a triangle.

"You see the news?" Dave began.

Ronson knew this wouldn't be a discussion of the new legislation but one of Dave's *jokes*, judging by the curvature of a smile which couldn't be dislodged from the corners of his mouth.

Dave continued: "There've been reports that a two-seater Cessna aircraft crashed in a Dublin cemetery yesterday afternoon. Police stated that one hundred and thirty-two bodies have been recovered so far, but that more were expected as crews worked through the night."

Jonas bent over the top of his spade, silently shaking.

Ronson felt emboldened by duty. "We'll have no casual racism here, Dave, please."

Dave shrugged. "It's traditional," he said. "Anyway, I'm a quarter Irish on my mother's side. Makes no difference to me. Just pick an ethnic group of your choice. The joke remains the same."

Ronson shook his head. "It's a matter of being respectful. Remember where you are." He gesticulated around them, no one in sight. "You never know who you might offend."

"Other than us everyone is dead."

"You know what I mean." Ronson shoved his hands into his coat pockets where they weren't any warmer.

Dave paused, as though deliberating whether to argue. Muttering something like *I was just saying*, he pushed the blade of his spade back into the soil.

Jonas took up the baton, as if one couldn't speak until the other had stopped. "I hear there'll be less work for us."

"How do you make that out?"

"Re-using graves. We won't have to dig so deep."

"It doesn't work like that. In those instances where remains are to be buried in existing graves without removal of the current incumbent the *lift and deepen* policy will apply. Yes, you'll be creating space for the new remains to be placed above the old ones, but first you'll need to dig a deeper hole, not simply place newer coffins closer to the surface."

Jonas considered this. "Chances are we'll encounter remains then. Where the coffins have rotted."

"That might be the case. I'm sure there's provision for it in your contracts."

"There's provision for a lot of things," piped up Dave. It was a retort which meant nothing, as all of them knew.

Ronson made a remark about it all coming out in the wash, then returned to his bicycle and cycled across to the section of the cemetery he had earmarked for the largest number of reclamations. Clouds concealed the sun, but the circle shone through; as though behind gauze, behind a shroud.

"If you're not happy, leave."

Ronson's wife lay on her front, a book sunk into a pillow, Ronson's hand rested on her rear.

"It's not as simple as that."

"Nothing ever is. Scratch my back."

Ronson gently clawed her white skin under the duvet.

"Up. Left. No, right. Down. There. There. That's it. No, back there. Not there. Never mind, I'll do it myself."

Ronson rolled onto his back. "It's not the job, it's the paperwork. Not only that, but I want to make sure I'm making the right decisions."

"None of *them* will complain."

Ronson sighed. "This isn't about *them*, is it? Well, it is; but it's about respect."

"All your decisions will be checked, won't they?"

"I imagine so."

"Well there you go, then. It won't be your final say-so."

No, thought Ronson, *I would only have been obeying orders.*

His wife closed her book, turned onto her side. They had been together twenty years and he could only tell that she'd aged through photographs. That's how the years deceived. Yet if they had been *apart* for twenty years he would have noticed the changes instantly.

Just for a moment, he imagined what she would look like dead.

"Let's make love." She buried a hand under the bedclothes.

The moment extrapolated across time.

Dawn was arriving earlier and earlier. Ronson's wife knew not to grumble as she sensed him leave the bed. She was done with cajoling. During the winter months he left and returned at more reasonable times. It was all swings and roundabouts, as her mother used to say. All the fun of the fair.

Ronson drove under the cover of darkness, as though a vampire racing against the rising of the sun. By the time he had unlocked the gates, the light had already begun to disappear the night. It was a cloudy morning; yesterday's sunshine had broached a cold night and the subsequent cover created wraiths of mist that might have unsettled some. Ronson never experienced trepidation or nervous excitement. Even when he first started working in the cemetery he wasn't daunted. Perhaps he had no imagination, but that could be a dangerous state of being. It meant he had to believe whatever it was that he saw.

He squinted into the mist. It had to be an illusion but a form coalesced within, like smoke blown into a clear glass.

He resisted the temptation to rub his eyes. That was the stuff of cliché. He glanced up at the sun, a pale *hostia*. Returning his gaze to the mist he watched as it was sucked backwards, the object within ravelling as though it were a laundry line caught up in the wheel of a low-flying aircraft. Within seconds the illusion was erased, the boundaries of reality regained. Ronson entered his office and popped bread into the toaster. A red glow penetrated the room with an exaggerated illusion of warmth, but it wasn't until his second cup of tea that he felt that warmth replicated inside.

He spent the morning with his right index finger running down a list of names and numbers, occasionally stopping and circling a Photostat copy of the same list. The recent amendment to Section 74 of the London Local Authorities Act 2007 empowered a burial authority to disturb or authorise the disturbance of human remains interred in a grave for the purpose of increasing the space for interments in the grave. Ronson reminded himself that the law was not only behind him, but propelling him. None of the graves he eventually selected would have been tended for many years. There might well be no living relatives. It was right and proper to utilise the space. Just as there was movement above the earth, so there had to be movement beneath it.

He put down his pen. That was just the case, wasn't it? Rarely did anyone move into a new home wondering how the previous occupant had lived. Lives did not overlap. Once one occupation ended, another started. That was the way of things.

Making the connection between graves and houses, Ronson recalled a recent interview with Dr Julie Rugg of the University of York's Cemetery Research Group: "A lot of people don't appreciate how deep graves can be," Rugg had said. "If you turn a cemetery upside down it looks like the middle of the city – like a skyscraper. In the UK, the common graves of the 19th century, for example, are very, very deep."

Ronson felt himself ease. Using that analogy, interring bodily remains deeper into the soil effectively moved them into a penthouse. It was an upwardly mobile solution. And anyway, who was there to object?

He ate beef paste sandwiches in the office with the door closed. From his position in the chair he had a clear view of the pathway leading to the older part of the cemetery, through the window set in the door. It was rare to glimpse a visitor in this direction, which is why he often took to facing it. Years ago the cemetery had been isolated in this direction. Only over the past seventy years had gravestones begun to surround the building, like American Indians circling a wagon train.

Ronson shook his head. He was getting as bad as Dave for inappropriate cultural references. He didn't strive for political correctness as some did, but he was sensitive to everyone's right to be treated equally.

And that was how he addressed the current task, wasn't it? Ensuring that no one was needlessly offended. It all came down to a question of taste.

There was movement along the pathway.

He sat straight. Narrowed his vision.

Something again, barely perceptible. Probably a rabbit.

A very tall rabbit.

Ronson stood, wishing he had spent some time cleaning that window.

The beef paste sat carpeting his tongue.

Again, something.

He walked to the door, opened it. The sun had burnt through the cloud cover, dappling light across the vegetation; the evergreens almost visibly absorbing chlorophyll, with the deciduous trees yearning to push their buds through stiffened fingers. There was nothing unusual. Ronson considered the possibility that he had witnessed an optical illusion as light refracted against the window, even as his legs took him down the steps and onto the pathway. He continued walking, his ears accumulating the sound of the breeze, the movement of the leaves, the birdsong, the faint echo of traffic. His movements were fluid, almost ethereal. After several minutes he reached the end of the pathway, which led in two directions around the older part of the cemetery, eventually meeting in a circle. He paused, listened. Nothing unusual. *Why should there be?* Ronson realised he still held his sandwich. He brought it to his mouth, bit.

He couldn't tell his wife that he had been spooked. He couldn't even tell himself.

"Don't forget we're seeing James and Mary at the weekend."

"What?"

"James and Mary. Remember?"

Ronson nodded. It was Wednesday, the weekend a far distant future.

He was reading an old article on the Guardian website regarding the lack of space in metropolitan cemeteries. The article postulated that around 55 million people died worldwide annually, which equated to around 0.8% of the world's population; although interestingly this was equivalent to 100% of England's. Ronson imagined the entire English population dying and being replaced on a yearly basis. What if there was only one location where people could die. Would people flock there, or would it be abandoned? How long would it take for England to be filled if it were assigned the sole destination for burials? He found these contemplations fascinating.

The article was out of date, given the new legislation, but it had predicted that London's cemeteries would be completely full within 20-30 years. Cremations weren't the solution. In many instances cemeteries still housed the urns, indefinitely; and cremation posed increased environmental problems of its own. Statistics suggested that the burning of dental fillings alone contributed to 15% of the UK's mercury emissions. Ronson raised this figure with his wife.

"I'm not going to say that this doesn't matter," she said, "because it does; but surely it doesn't matter to you?"

Ronson ran a hand through his hair. "The dead outnumber the living. For the majority of human history that's always been the case. And they're ever increasing. New ways have to be introduced to deal with that the issue."

"And that's what you're doing, right? You're part of the solution, not part of the problem. You're doing what you can, but you can't reverse the process."

Ronson nodded. His wife said something else, but he had stopped listening. He was struck by the thought that at some point – in mankind's long forgotten past – the living would have outnumbered the dead. Who was the first bona fide Homo sapien to have died? What an astonishing consideration. Almost at once the question seemed an important one to answer.

Good luck with that.

"What?"

"I said, 'good luck with that'." His wife sensed his confusion. "With sorting the cemetery. What did you think I was talking about?"

Ronson didn't know.

The time was shortly after four am. The night had been saturated with heat. Ronson had barely slept. They had opened all the windows, and he had woken to find his wife sleeping at the opposite end of the bed, her feet near his head. Four months had passed since the change in legislation, and work was due to start that morning on lifting and deepening the first selection of graves earmarked by Ronson. He had begun to feel ambivalent about the whole process, now the idea was assimilated into the everyday. No burials were scheduled, it was simply the start of the clearing process. There would be instances when work might be interrupted. The graves couldn't be cleared on an as and when basis, but en masse. The preliminaries had been overseen and authorised by his superiors in the council, but once again the day to day running of the cemetery remained his responsibility.

The previous few days had seen protests at the cemetery gates by those who – Ronson believed – held ill-informed opinions. Thankfully, they weren't inclined to arrive at sunrise as he was, and his interactions with them were minor. By the time it came to closing the cemetery, they had already packed up and gone home.

The newspapers had validated his choices. No living relatives had come forward to raise objections to the graves he had highlighted. The Catholic Church had also expressed a nationwide opinion that re-interring remains deeper in the same grave did not constitute an exhumation. In many instances, they had adopted this practice for some years. If any ghosts of doubt remained in Ronson's mind, they were shadows of what he might label a *respectful unease*. An almost arbitrary sensation linked to historical consciousness; something that should be discarded in today's world.

The local newspaper had also dispensed with the word, *decimate*. Someone – not Ronson – had written to the paper bemoaning the use of the term, stating that they believed it meant to *kill* one in ten and couldn't be used in relation to those already dead. Ronson had done some research over the term himself, finding it of Roman origin where one in ten soldiers in a legion might be killed as punishment for the whole group. Briefly, the word *punishment* had lingered at the back of his mind, but under no circumstances could his choice of graves be considered as punishment. His selection had been fair and without bias; to his knowledge, he had no connection to any of those chosen.

As usual, he stood at the office doorway, watching daylight break like an egg over a painting by Goya. The warmer weather had chased away illusion. He had almost forgotten those few instances of aberration where his imagination had made a fool out of him. Under the glare of the summer sun, headstones gleamed as though freshly minted and he was reminded of the term *the marble orchard*, as a cemetery descriptor. Not because those grave markers might bear fruit, but because of their arrangement in rows like planted trees.

Ronson waited until night shadows were replaced by those of the sun, then walked back to his desk where his list of graves waited. He had isolated exactly 2,000, a not inconsiderable task. These were grouped into date order. Work would begin on four of them that day. Jonas had been right in some respects – the grave-digging had been franchised out to accommodate the extra work, which meant that Dave and Jonas had unfortunately been laid off. Ronson felt a pang of regret about this, although none of it had been his decision. He half expected to have found them picketing the cemetery gates, before realising they both had more respect for the location – and for themselves – than he ever credited them with.

He tapped his pen. His peccadillo for catching the sunrise often meant there were several hours to kill during the summer months before he was officially employed, and often he spent these sleeping or catching up on some reading. Today, though, was shrill with anticipation at those first works, and despite his best efforts Ronson found he couldn't sit still. He decided to enjoy the momentary quiet and go for a walk.

He left at the rear of the building, intending to make a full circuit so that by the time he was done he would be in the oldest part of the cemetery and possibly ready to greet those workers for the interments. Amongst the newer graves, cut flowers jostled for attention with the wild and planted varieties adorning the grassy areas. Even there, the distinction between the dead and the living was evident. Ronson walked slowly, enjoying the sun on his back, the birdsong tinkering with the air. He stopped and read some of the recent inscriptions. Word count and content was now heavily restricted compared to the epitaphs of years before, but as usual he was touched by the sometimes shortness of time between birth and death dates, or even through the proletariat simplicity of flowers spelling out *Mummy*.

And as he walked he was struck with the knowledge that

these recent graves would also one day be subsumed by others, that the memories of those who tended them would fail and rot, that eventually they would be forgotten. Not for the first time he envisaged his own grave; childless, he knew it wouldn't be tended long, and probably never should his wife die before him. Despite the radiance of the sun, he suddenly couldn't shake off the prescience of darkness, and as he wandered across to the older section of the cemetery the insistence of death weighed each successive step.

Ronson's first thought when he saw the group was that the workers had arrived early, perhaps deliberately so in order to avoid any local press or objectors. But the absence of hi-vis jackets shouldered a concern and – coupled with the realisation that he had yet to unlock the gates – gave him thought that these were in fact the protestors, who had no doubt sneaked in via the tree branches that overhung the railings. Irrepressible annoyance coursed through him. This was unfair. He was not to blame for the situation and the inevitable confrontation would do more to disturb the dead than the carefully managed restructuring could accomplish.

He picked up his pace, unsure what course of action to take. Perhaps he should ignore the interlopers until reinforcements arrived. Representatives from the council were due to attend the first sessions, as well as the workers themselves. There was safety in numbers. Ronson did not need to be isolated, but then he knew that neither should he be intimidated. He had worked with great respect with the legislation. He loved his work. He loved the cemetery. No one could argue with that.

So he pressed on.

Two hundred yards off, he realised there were more of them than he first thought. Their numbers appeared to be replicating, as though one stepped from behind the shadow of another behind the shadow of another. Ronson knew it had to be perspective: that section of cemetery stretched out for some distance, and the circular pathway would conceal more than it revealed. Yet something made him slow his pace. Perhaps he should turn back. The group would have its own dynamic, which usually differed from that of individuals. But this was *his* territory, he couldn't shirk responsibility.

Again, he stepped up the pace. Birdsong intensified around him as though an outward manifestation of his resolve. There was a rush to the day. To his right, a small family of rabbits played openly. Ronson's shoes kicked gravel in his stride. Sweat ran a course down the small of his back. The sun had fully risen, depleting the final vestiges of night. Ronson realised the group was now clearly visible. Then he balked again. They were in costume. Ronson wasn't a historian, but a glut of BBC dramas enabled him to identify Victorian clothing. He found himself slowing, before a *gentle pressure* began to propel him onwards. His senses reeled. Instinctively he dug his heels into the path, but there was no stopping that subtle coercion. His destiny lay with the group.

Ronson had never experienced genuine fear but he did now. Closing his eyes heightened anxiety. It was no way to exist. With considerable resolve he stopped contemplating the machinations of his movements and found that acceptance led to relaxation. There was a honeyed, sepia photograph-feel to the group. He no longer doubted that these were ghosts. With each blink their number increased until there must have been over a thousand. Yet these were not open-mouthed, cack-eyed ghouls, but a representation of a long-lost community. They didn't reach out to him with bony fingers, seeking to clutch him into the earth – their flesh was as his – and their expressions were infused with gratitude.

Barely ten feet away each of them recognised, catalogued, and acknowledged him, just as respectfully as he had been when searching for their names, family histories, identities. Close-up, their presence became ephemeral, and as he was passed from one to another their number reduced until out of two thousand only a handful remained. Ronson slipped into a dream-like state – a mental buoyancy – whilst remaining conscious that he wasn't dreaming. He caught snatches of whispered conversations:

Thank you.

You remembered us.

Thank you.

You remembered us.

When Ronson woke he found he had been placed on a mound of grass, with his head raised slightly higher than the rest of his body. He immediately stood. Looking down at the ground he half-expected to see a headstone with his name carved black within the marble, but there was nothing to indicate this was a grave.

He looked around. Near the closed cemetery gates he saw a handful of the group pass through the railings. Their number had been decimated, but it was less of a punishment than a kind of reward. Somehow, Ronson's decision-making had been an act of supplication, of redemption for a lucky few. The cemetery had been an orchard after all. By some curious twist of fate, it had borne fruit.

Ronson walked slowly around the graves, nodding at those where he had placed green triangles. He felt an affiliation with those beneath the soil. A bond had been forged amongst the forgotten. Looking at his watch he saw that little time had passed since he began his walk. There were still a few hours before he would open the gates and admit protestors or contractors or both. Reluctantly he returned to the office, the building seemingly now out of place within this quiet haven. Ronson made himself a cup of tea and stood in the doorway, preternaturally calm.

Twisted Limerick 10

Ramsey Campbell

If you've thawed out an alien thing
There's a perfect opponent to bring.
When a sentient carrot
Encounters a parrot
It's Poll who will prove to be king.

About the Authors

James Barclay is mainly an author and sometimes an actor. He is the author of two linked trilogies and a stand-alone concerning fantasy cult heroes *The Raven*, and also from the same world, his popular *Elves* trilogy. He has also written an epic fantasy duology, *The Ascendants of Estorea*, and two novellas: *Light Stealer* and *Vault of Deeds*. He has recently published his thirteenth novel, the military fantasy, *Heart of Granite*. Recent acting credits include 'Jeff' in *Jeffrey Bernard is Unwell* and 'Major Courtney' in *The Ladykillers*. He lives very happily in Teddington with his wife, Clare, two noisy boys and an equally noisy dog.

In 2015 **Ramsey Campbell** received the Lifetime Achievement World Fantasy Award and an Honorary Fellowship from Liverpool John Moores University for outstanding services to literature. His most recent books are *The Booking, The Searching Dead* and *Limericks of the Alarming and Phantasmal*. He can be found online at: www.ramseycampbell.com/

Simon Clark has written many short stories and novels, including *Darkness Demands, Blood Crazy, Vampyrrhic, Secrets of the Dead,* and *The Night of the Triffids*, which continues John Wyndham's classic *The Day of the Triffids. The Night of the Triffids* has also been adapted as a full-cast audio drama by Big Finish, subsequently broadcast by the BBC. Simon lives in Yorkshire, England. His website is www.nailedbytheheart.com

Edward Cox is the author of The Relic Guild Trilogy published by Gollancz. He used to lecture in creative writing and write reviews, but he's over all that now and spends most of his time pretending to be a ghost.

Andrew Hook has over 130 short stories in print, alongside several books. His most recent titles include the neo-noir crime novels *The Immortalists* and *Church Of Wire* (Telos Publishing). 2016 will see the publication of his fifth short story collection *Human Maps* (Eibonvale) and a SF/F/H hybrid novella "The Greens" (Snowbooks).

Paul Kane is the award-winning, bestselling author and editor of over 60 books – including the sellout *Hooded Man* (Arrowhead trilogy omnibus), *Hellbound Hearts*, *Lunar* (set to be turned into a feature film, scripted by Paul), *Monsters*, *Blood RED* and *Sherlock Holmes & The Servants of Hell* from Solaris. Find out more at www.shadow-writer.co.uk

Maura McHugh lives in Ireland, and her short fiction and essays have appeared in publications in America and Europe, as well as two collections – *Twisted Fairy Tales* and *Twisted Myths* – published in the USA. She's written several comic book series, including co-writing *Witchfinder* for Dark Horse Comics. She's also a screenwriter, playwright, a critic, and has served on the juries of international literary, comic book, and film awards. Her website is http://splinister.com and she tweets as @splinister

Sarah Pinborough is a critically acclaimed, award-winning, adult and YA author. She is also a screenwriter who has written for the BBC and has several original television projects in development. Her next novel, *Behind Her Eyes*, coming from HarperFiction in the UK and Flatiron in the US (January 2017), has sold in nearly twenty territories worldwide and is a dark thriller about relationships with a kicker of a twist. You can follow her on Twitter @sarahpinborough

Lynda E. Rucker is an American writer now living in Europe. She has sold more than thirty short stories to various magazines and anthologies, won the 2015 Shirley Jackson Award for Best

Short Story, and is a regular columnist for *Black Static*. Her first collection, *The Moon Will Look Strange*, was released in 2013 from Karōshi Books, and Swan River Press published her second, *You'll Know When You Get There*, in 2016.

Michael Marshall Smith is a novelist and screenwriter. Under this name he has published over eighty short stories and four novels – *Only Forward, Spares, One of Us* and *The Servants* – winning the Philip K. Dick, International Horror Guild, and August Derleth awards, along with the Prix Bob Morane in France. He has won the British Fantasy Award for Best Short Fiction four times, more than any other author. Writing as **Michael Marshall**, he has published seven internationally-bestselling thrillers including The Straw Men series, *The Intruders* – recently a BBC series starring John Simm and Mira Sorvino – and *Killer Move*. His most recent novel is *We Are Here*. He lives in Santa Cruz, California, with his wife, son, and two cats.

Mark West lives in Northamptonshire with his wife Alison and their young son Matthew. Since discovering the small press in 1998 he has published over eighty short stories, two novels, a novelette, a chapbook, a collection and three novellas (one of which, *Drive*, was nominated for a British Fantasy Award). Away from writing, he enjoys reading, walking, and playing Dudeball with his son. He can be contacted through his website at www.markwest.org.uk and is also on Twitter as @MarkEWest

Now We Are Ten

Edited by

Ian Whates

Celebrating the first ten years of NewCon Press
With sixteen original stories written especially for this book

Contents:

Available as a signed limited edition hardback, paperback, and eBook

www.newconpress.co.uk

NEWCON PRESS

Splinters of Truth
Storm Constantine

Storm Constantine is one of our finest writers of genre fiction. This new collection, **Splinters of Truth**, features fifteen stories, four of them original to this volume, that transport the reader to richly imagined realms one moment and shine a light on our own world's darkest corners the next. A writer of rare passion, Storm delivers here some of her most accomplished work to date.

"Constantine's talent for twisting the mundane and making it dark and delicious shines out on each page"
— *Starburst*

Cover art by Danielle Lainton

"Storm Constantine is a myth-making Gothic queen. Her stories are poetic, involving, delightful and depraved. I wouldn't swap her for a dozen Anne Rices." – *Neil Gaiman*

"Storm Constantine… is a daring romantic sensualist, as well as a fine storyteller." – *Poppy Z Brite*

"Storm Constantine is a literary fantasist of outstanding power and originality. Her work is rich, idiosyncratic and completely engaging. Her themes have much in common with Philip K Dick – the nature of identify, the nature of reality, the creative power of the human imagination – while her sensibility reminds me of Angela Carter at her most inventive." – *Michael Moorcock*

Available now from NewCon Press
www.newconpress.co.uk

Secret Language
Neil Williamson

Following on from the success of Neil's debut novel *The Moon King* (runner up for the BSFA Award behind Ann Leckie and shorlisted for the British Fantasy Holdstock Award), **Secret Language** gathers together sixteen stories, four of them written especially for this collection, that demonstrate why he is one of genre fiction's finest writers. The BSFA shortlisted story "Arrhythmia" provides just one of the highlights, and while all four of the new stories are excellent, one in particular, "The Death of Abigail Goudy" may just be the best thing Neil has ever written.

"Williamson's territories are the liminal experience and the murky corners of the psyche. He is a virtuoso of the fleeting glimpse, a laureate of loss." – *Interzone*

"With a few deft swipes of the writing brush, Williamson conjures an entire universe… If Williamson is speaking a secret language it is one that resonates, surprises and entertains." – *Bristol Book Blog*

"Williamson nails style and structure to tell of high school hackers heisting music on the streets to create their own mixes." – *Speculation (of 'Pearl in the Shell')*

"Williamson is one of the best Scottish short story writers alive today." – *Jim Steel*

TALES OF THE APT

SPOILS OF WAR
Adrian Tchaikovsky

Tales of the Apt is a companion series to the best-selling decalogy *Shadows of the Apt* (Tor UK) by 2016 Arthur C. Clarke Award winning author Adrian Tchaikovsky. It gathers together short stories from disparate places and supplements them with a wealth of new tales written especially for the series. Together, they combine to provide a different perspective, an alternative history that parallels and unfolds alongside the familiar one, filling in the gaps and revealing intriguing backstories for established characters. A must read for any fan of the *Shadows of the Apt* books, where epic fantasy meets steampunk and so much more.

"The whole Shadows of the Apt series has been one of the most original creations in modern fantasy" – *Upcoming4.me*

"Tchaikovsky makes a good and enjoyable mix between a medieval-looking world and the presence of technology" – *Starburst Magazine*

Available now from NewCon Press
www.newconpress.co.uk

Immanion Press
Speculative Fiction

Dark in the Day, Ed. by Storm Constantine & Paul Houghton

Weirdness lurks beyond the margins of the mundane, emerging to dismantle our assumptions of reality. Dark in the Day is an anthology of weird fiction, penned by established writers and also those new to the genre – the latter being authors who are, or were, students of Creative Writing at Staffordshire University, where editor Storm Constantine occasionally delivers guest lectures. Her co-editor, Paul Houghton, is the senior lecturer in Creative Writing at the university.

Contributors include: Martina Bellovičová, J. E. Bryant, Glynis Charlton, Storm Constantine, Louise Coquio, Elizabeth Counihan, Krishan Coupland, Elizabeth Davidson, Siân Davies, Paul Finch, Rosie Garland, Rhys Hughes, Kerry Fender, Andrew Hook, Paul Houghton, Tanith Lee, Tim Pratt, Nicholas Royle, Michael Marshall Smith, Paula Wakefield, Ian Whates and Liz Williams.
ISBN: 978-1-907737-74-9 £11.99, $18.99

Animate Objects by Tanith Lee

There is no such thing as an inanimate object… And how could that be? Because, simply, everything is formed from matter, and basically, at *root*, the matter that makes up everything in the physical world – the Universe – is of the same substance. Which means, on that basic level, we – you, me, and that power station over there – are all the exact riotous, chaotic, amorphous *same*. Here is an assortment of Lee takes on the nature, and perhaps intentions, of so-called non-sentient things. And you're quite safe. This is only a book. An inanimate object.

From the Introduction by Tanith Lee

The original hardback of this collection, of which there were only 35 copies, was published by Immanion Press in 2013, to commemorate Tanith Lee receiving the Lifetime Achievement Award at World Fantasycon. It included 5 previously unpublished pieces. This new release includes a further 2 stories, co-written by Tanith Lee and John Kaiine, and new interior illustrations by Jarod Mills.
ISBN: 978-1-907737-73-2, £11.99 $18.99

Para Animalia Edited by Storm Constantine & Wendy Darling

 Based on the world created by Storm Constantine for her Wraeththu novels, the stories in this collection explore how various Wraeththu tribes interact with animals, have spiritual or working relationships with them, or have encountered zoological mysteries out in the world. From the wolves of frozen forests, and a har's obsession with spiders, to the snakes of parched deserts and the hunting dogs of what was once the African plains, hara confront a strengthening natural world that is now free of humanity.

'Para Animalia' features stories from nine writers, some of whom are well known within Wraeththu fandom and/or have written Wraeththu Mythos novels published by Immanion Press. Also included are two new stories each by Storm Constantine and Wendy Darling.

ISBN: 978-1-907737-70-1 £11.99, $18.99

Night's Nieces: the Legacy of Tanith Lee

 In the footsteps of the High Priestess of Fantasy... Tanith Lee was a huge influence on fantasy literature, and a generation of writers were captivated by her iconic prose and surreal visions. Here is a collection of stories by female writers, for whom Tanith Lee was a friend and mentor, and an inspiration. Each 'niece' has written a short story inspired by Tanith's work, as well as an accompanying article. The book, edited by Storm Constantine, also includes previously unpublished photographs from Tanith's life, as well as artwork by the authors.

Contributors include Storm Constantine, Cecilia Dart-Thornton, Vera Nazarian, Sarah Singleton, Kari Sperring, Sam Stone, Freda Warrington and Liz Williams. With an introduction by John Kaiine.

ISBN: 978-1-907737-71-8 £11.99 $18.99

Immanion Press
http://www.immanion-press.com
info@immanion-press.com

www.ingramcontent.com/pod-product-compliance
Lightning Source LLC
Chambersburg PA
CBHW030255270626
47156CB00022B/2773